Janet Frame   *Photo by Anne Noble*

Janet Frame was born in Dunedin, New Zealand, in 1924, and has been writing all her life. Her work includes ten novels, among them *Owls Do Cry, State of Siege, Yellow Flowers in the Antipodean Room, Faces in the Water* (The Women's Press, 1980) and *Living in the Maniototo* (The Women's Press, 1981); also four collections of stories and sketches, a volume of poetry and a children's book, *Mona Minim and the Smell of the Sun*. Janet Frame has been a Burns Scholar, won the New Zealand Scholarship in Letters and the Hubert Church Award for prose, was awarded an honorary Doctorate in Literature by the University of Otago, and in 1980 won the Fiction Prize, New Zealand Book Awards, for *Living in the Maniototo*.

Janet Frame is recognised as New Zealand's finest living novelist, and *Living in the Maniototo* was hailed as 'near a masterpiece' (*Daily Telegraph*), and 'the most original and resourceful novel I have read for a long time' (*New Statesman*).

Janet Frame
Scented Gardens
for the Blind

The Women's Press

Published by The Women's Press Limited 1982
A member of the Namara Group
34 Great Sutton Street, London EC1V 0DX

Reprinted in 1986

First published by George Braziller, Inc
1 Park Avenue, New York, NY 10016 USA

This is a work of fiction. Any resemblance
to persons living or dead is purely coincidental.

British Library Cataloguing in Publication Data

    Frane, Janet
      Scented gardens for the blind.
      I Title
      823$^{(F)}$ PR9639.3.F4
      ISBN 0-7043-3899-8

Printed in Great Britain by Nene Litho
and bound by Woolnough Bookbinding
both of Irthlingborough, Northants

1

Erlene is in the next room. She sits, like a blind person, in the dark. I have acquired the habit of listening intently to her silence, set in the midst of the pitched volume of darkness, the gong of daylight, the creak and settle of furniture, the steady low white tone of windows, the scatterbrain fluttering of curtains, the deep sighs of beds which grind and ache from the stress and turmoil of human bodies. All sounds have been amplified since my daughter lost her power of speech; yet if I knew that her first words were to be judgment upon me I would kill her, I would go now to the little room where she sits alone in the dark, and kill her, and she would not be able to cry for help.

When I was a child, in this very town, I had a little friend on stalks, and she was called Poppy; she was velvet, and we walked together to school every day, and put our hands through the hedges and fences, cadging flowers, a red and pink and yellow stained assortment juicy and warm in our hands. And whenever Poppy and I met, we talked and talked, because we were friends. But if by chance in our walking (we always walked in step), we got out of step or we separated with Poppy going one side of the lamppost and I, Vera, going the other, the curse of silence was put upon us.

"We have got the pip," Poppy would tell me. "I have got the pip with you and you have got the pip with me."

And we shut our mouths tight, and all day for years we did not speak, only stared at each other, judging, judging, and I could see my crimes like clear glittering pictures in Poppy's eyes.

Cut flowers last longer, I am told, if they are bruised or singed or if you crumble in the water one or two of those pills which people swallow to deaden a continual feeling of pain.

So I placed before me a diagram of the human head neck and chest, drawn to scale, with the tunnels of speech and breath so gay in their scarlet lining; and ignoring the arrows darting from right and left to stab at the listed names of the blue and red and pink territory, I moved my finger, walked it along the corridor, trying to find the door into speech, but the diagram did not show it, somewhere in the brain, the book said, an impulse in the brain letting the words go free, sympathetic movement of larynx lips tongue, the shaping of breath, and even then, the book said, it may not be speech which emerges, it may only be a cry such as a bird makes or a beast lurking in the trees at night, or, loneliest of all, not the cry of a bird or beast but the first uttering of a new language which is understood by no one and nothing, and which causes a smoke screen of fear to cloud the mind, as defense against the strangeness.

10

The animal claws, too, slide from their sheath. The new language must be destroyed or driven back to its birthplace in silence and darkness.

The plan of speech comforted me. I kept it under my pillow at night, hoping for a miracle, in the way a child keeps its tooth, its first milk-white perfect plan of pain, and expects the granting of a wish, like the death of an aunt or parent or brother or sister, or the public bestowal of love, presents or holidays by the red-ink teacher in the infant school, or adventurous blindness, a magnet on the other side of the light, withdrawing the sun, the buttercups, ragwort, yellow pansies.

I began a furtive seeking for cures. I listened on corners to the folk doctors. It was useless to tell myself that I had been educated and was therefore not superstitious, when grief, panic, bewilderment, acting like a sponge, had seemed to absorb my knowledge and reason as if they were but temporary stains upon the fabric of feeling. If blind moles, silk-eared bats, dragons, had inhabited my country I would have searched for them north south east west on plains and mountains and deep beneath moss, stone and seabed. I would have made potions from dragons' blood, glitter dust from the bodies of bats, in my ritual standing not upon heaths or moors but upon this antipodean beach by a Pacific sea sprayed with light from the ripe, squeezed, bitter sun.

I pored over an old yellow-leaved book. Speech, loss of. The bowels must be kept open, the skin clear, the eyes bright. The closed bowel signified the incarceration of man within himself. The yellow-leaved book explained panic measures of leverage, unlocking, breaking and entering.

The speech will be clear, beautiful, the words pleasurably patterned like daisy chains, with biting links, with the smell of the earth and the sun and the juice of man. But what is the use of speech? On and on, saying nothing, the tattered bargain-price words, the great red-flagged sale of trivialities, the shutdown sellout of the mind?

My life has boundaries; I have discovered the exact amount of earth which I need; death will return me at the exact moment to my own door; my share is small and deep; it does not include a trek of the world, a visit overseas to Edward who travels fast, changing trains, planes, generations. My life is accomplished in this small town, almost in this one street in this house where I live as a hermit while in the next room, claiming space and time with her powers of silence, my daughter sits speechless, a living fable, with no spinning wheel to prick her finger upon, dropping blood to the snow, no underground stream where at midnight the old soldier will ferry her to the palace for dancing and in the morning I shall strike her in anger, seeing her shoes worn to holes. She does not sift beans in the ashes. There are no conditions for a miracle. We have only a hazel tree which leans over the creek, having suffered the attacks of people who could not decide whether to leave it growing, since it bore little fruit, or to kill it in revenge for its barrenness. Its limbs are chipped and chopped; one is dead; on one branch there are three tiny hazelnuts snug in their green skin; shake shake hazel tree gold and silver over me. I need a fable to fall like a gentle cloak from the sky, to protect my daughter and myself with the cloth spread over the familiar names and situations, however terrible —the cutting out of tongues, metamorphoses, the removal of limbs, of the head turned smiling in the direction of the clock running bright like water.

Who is to blame?

Erlene must be prevented from telling the truth about me. A splash of violence, of blood pouring like rain upon my neat floral domed and buttoned shroud. I move; there are spiders in me, in the hollow of my arm where it is still joined to my body; yet my arm moves to protect the growing woman who was once aged five with a family of rosy-faced dolls with blue eyes and dark sweeping lashes which permitted and beautified sleep. And there was a nodule, like a compass, sewn in their bellies, and pressure there encouraged their mouths to say Mama Mama, or so it was believed, but a fault in the mechanism called forth a plaintive cry sounding strangely from their plump bodies, like the cry of a beggar on the street corner of a foreign city.

Her silence endangers me; it confuses me; I have

raised my voice when speaking to her, as if she were deaf. I have cut up the meat upon her dinner plate, as if she had lost the use of her hands. Sometimes I have found myself taking her arm, guiding her, as if she were blind. And when others in the town learned of her disability their trick of comfort was a similar confusion of the senses, the shift of emphasis from speech to sight, hearing, or the power of movement.

"At least there's consolation in knowing she's not blind," they said. Or, "Just think if she were deaf. Or crippled."

And none failed to put the question, "It's a good thing she is not also . . . so to speak . . . so to speak . . . is she?"

They meant abnormal. Divisions of the kind were fashionable at that time, and it was so easy to stifle one's need to help by deciding that help could neither be accepted nor understood. I have seen a quick-drying paint advertised lately in the shops. It is most convenient; it dries immediately it is brushed upon the wall. It is like habit, except that habit sets even more quickly upon the mind, and one is grateful for this convenience, the way it removes the need for laborious action or thought. And so we have grouped the deaf, dumb, blind, crippled, mentally ill, in one mass in order to "deal with" them, for we must "deal with" these vast surfaces of strangeness which demand all our lives a protective varnish of sympathy.

Protective for us; against them and ourselves. It is easy

14

to ward off their demands for patient understanding by obliterating them with a mass dull coat of generality.

All the same, I agreed with people who tried to console me.

"Yes," I said, "it would be terrible if she had been struck blind instead of dumb."

But to their fugal so-to-speak so-to-speak I gave no answer.

I deprived myself of each of my senses. It was I who was blind. I was threatened by the dreadful mass neighborhood of objects which acquire a power of mobility as soon as one loses one's sight, as if it were only the fact of being seen which keeps them in their place and now that they are free from the supervision of human eyes they may swoop, sway, dance, surround, always pursuing, threatening, trying to insinuate themselves in the dark, seeking their revenge for the withdrawal of the generosity, the benevolence of the glance of human eyes; for our gaze is always generous, it lingers, it follows the shape of the furniture, signs its approval along the dotted line of light surrounding each object; our sight keeps open house, plays host to all lovely or distorted forms, flatters each guest by granting an inevitable place within an image of wholeness; our pattern-crazy sight, rich, ambitious, loving, includes the dustbin and the sky, allows and admits the pertinence of all substance and shadow.

And no one knows how much the world is worn out, defaced, by the continual rubbing of human sight upon its edges, corners and open pages.

When one is blind, all that once seemed solid now flows and pursues. The day, like a lift out of control, sweeps up and down stopping at all floors of darkness. One longs more than ever to keep the world in its place, to demand that furniture should be seen and not heard, speak only when it is spoken to. But perhaps I am mistaken, perhaps our sight is not the perfect host, it is merely the owner of the house trying to make the best of entertaining this furious gate-crasher, light, which, denied the shelter and sustenance of being seen, will persist at the doors of other senses, queuing at the house of touch and hearing and smell and the unnamed senses which absorb the world, as some creatures absorb food, through the skin and through the invisible sponges on the shores of the mind which suck in the experience of time and are sought each night by the beachcombing dreams which also pick up the pawa shells, the lamp shells, the snail houses.

Light must get in, at all costs. Light will commit murder to get in. It is no use boarding up the house with blindness. One can pour darkness over the house until a thick layer sets, impenetrable as death, a concrete refusal, numbness, isolation; yet inside one meets light in every room, sitting by the fire, at home.

When people moved about me I found that they left

their shape in the air, as if they had been wearing the air as clothing which stayed molded even after they struggled out of it, for make no mistake, one struggles out of air because always it fits too tightly, ever since the first tight squeeze of it zipped into the lungs at the first breath, pinching at the tongue and the throat and setting up the cry which some take as a sign of admission into life but which is really only a protest that from the first moment of living the air does not fit, it has just not been made to measure, and all future breaths will cause pinching and pain, and how many times until death and nakedness will one be forced to cut off parts of oneself, to whittle at, mutilate the whole in order to accommodate the intransigent shape of air?

I was surrounded by shadows and presences. At first I used to put out my hands to prevent the attack. Then I would clutch an article of furniture, trying by force to keep it in its place, yet knowing that after I had withdrawn my hand the same terrible flowing and surrounding would continue. How I wished that the map of my room were in numbered segments which would stay pinned and numbered! And what gratitude I felt when I once carried a chair, and all the time I carried it, it stayed obediently in my grasp, and I could feel it surrendering without protest to the fact of its new position near the window; there was no rebellion; at last I felt I had gained control by touch. But how could I control the sun and the sky? I could not touch them. I had not wanted to control them before I became blind, but now I wondered how much the activities of the sun and the sky were the result of their being gazed at by human eyes. I had a primitive feeling that because I was now blind the sun might fall from the sky or the earth might stop spinning. I felt so powerless. Even the concept of power, as if it had been a solid substance, lost its proportion and ruling. I believed, in my powerless state, that I had once been in control of the world or that at least in some mysterious way with my neat, open, two eyes charged with the wisdom, discretion, command of sight, I had helped to fix the sun and the sky in their right place. Now, even in the daytime, in full summer, when I had no reason to believe that the sun was not shining, I felt cold in my darkness, I shivered, I wore a thick cardigan over my summer dress.

My senses were overlapping, misplaced.

I was afraid.

I listened.

The traffic lights showed red. The world would stop spinning. What color was red? A plaited squeeze from a tube of light, soaked in blood; or the dried pool of blood inside the door, the hasty obliteration of guilt; or the chair red with blood; no wonder the chair was the first object of furniture to submit to the new authority of my blindness; the chair habitually submissive, close to love and death and the bad smells of the human body; in and out of fashion. The chairs in our house are tall-backed, with bars, and webbing beneath the seat, with uncurled springs hanging; these are kitchen chairs; red with blood; submit, submit, torture, leveled secrets, primitive disclosures; dark-brown chairs stained with people.

The knots, hollows and joints of our lives, like wood, which matures and darkens, exposed to weather. Edward has not lived here for eleven years, yet the layers of life which peel from us from time to time like discarded skins still stay attached to the furniture which Edward used. During the months I was blind I could feel and identify the layers left by him; I could even separate them, shuffle and sift them, with a touch of my fingers; but I could never quite remove them or detach the invisible hinge which held them to the surface of chairs, tables, floors, walls. Sometimes, walking blindly in the house, I stumbled across objects which had not been there when I could see, and for a while I could not understand the nature of them; some were crushed beneath my feet; others pierced my skin and I could feel the drops of blood at my ankle. Surely when I could see I had not such difficulty in walking across a floor! Then I realized gradually that I walked through accumulations of four lives—my own, Edward's, Erlene's, and my father's; and the wonder was not that these accumulations had suddenly made themselves palpable, but that I had been able to move through them at all. They might have held me prisoner by their very weight and mass.

But the traffic lights stayed at red. Red and yellow were the colors which did not become dim in my memory. Red blazed across the neutral screens of my eyes, which, at first, I kept opening and closing suddenly as if to surprise my power of sight in case it lurked near, waiting to seize its chance of readmission. Got you, I said, snapping open my eyes and staring at the dark, and then quickly putting out my hand I would feel for the wall or the table or some other article of furniture, and touch it, and a warmth which I never knew belonged to such objects would flow into my fingers and along my arm, through my whole body; a sun-colored light invading at all costs. I could not think of yellow as an independent color. Yellow was the sun. Of course. Did I not once control it? The sun, the shadow of a buttercup, a yellow stone, a beetle with a calico back, the tall pennyflowers, snubs of broom and gorse, jerseyed bees footballing in a wild seasonal scrum, pregnant hay, heaving and spreading, leaned in a corner of a paddock.

So I stayed blind, biting my way through the light, sniffing, touching, staring at the darkness, waiting for it to topple into light. I had to believe the sun. But when I heard people exclaim, The sun's bright today, isn't it nice in the sun, I realized that it wasn't anymore my visiting relation, that I couldn't care anymore whether it wiped its yellow feet on the front-door mat—how could I care when its only entry now was illegal and secret, with murder done, guilt endured, and that great acre of blood surging which I had to pretend had no attribute but redness when all the time I knew the commotion of seas' thunder swish crash sorting out the deep graveyard where light is dim and green; I hear blood. I shut my door of seeing, locked it, and turned to listen, and the first sound was blood. I could not escape from the tumult; drums, parades, congregations of scarlet; the red horses prancing in the night, in the storm. Who is whispering? I could not escape from the gossiping blood, the secrets gathered at all corners of the flesh-and-bone highways, the foretelling of worms with bracelets, in white lace dresses, dancing a Maypole, plait and stitch around each bone; circulation, pamphlets of death, obscene publishings, rumors; the terrible babbling of blood. It was only the light, stirring and stirring with its dazzling spurtle at my cauldron of hearing; it was my other sense at the boil, overflowing, but gradually settling to an habitual simmer as I grew used to my blindness and learned to ignore the telltale demands of my blood, and began to listen to the sounds which came from beyond myself, though at first I could not be sure, and as soon as a sound reached my ears I would quickly touch some part of my body, as one does to exterminate an insect which may have crawled from the

21

layers of skin, or may have flown from the surrounding involvement of air; soon I learned to distinguish and enjoy the festival flying in of sound from beyond myself, and was grateful when it reached me, arriving like an insect, a ladybird, a homing pigeon carrying its message curled within a tiny silver ring.

In the end I gave up trying to see, for even when one becomes blind there is a long interval during which one strives to see, although knowing it to be useless; chasing will-o'-the-wisps of remembered color, casting out this way and that, the ravaged nets of vision in the hope of trapping a wing of blue (what is blue?), green; remembering in despair the vapored color breathed from the skin of every shape. But I remembered more often the sound of color, the surface of it, oranges tar-sealed with golden tar, steamrolled under the sun with its engine working; hear the sun? the grind and struggle of light steam-powered, then the rush of thought past one's ears, trying to catch the traveler who is invisible, riding the metaphor of its own speed, leaving only a taste of time —sweet, sour.

Light. The houses beaming their messages along the coast. All day hammers beating upon wood, iron, steel; flattening, molding, distorting, driving home the lesson. The train struggling up the hill, its groan, hiss, joyous whistle, Got It, Got It, if only it hadn't been raining and the wheels were not turning in the same place, slipping, rabbit squeak, the sigh from the chest coughing out the sooty sediment in the oiled lungs, whoosh, a shriek; unlike the new Diesel cry which blares on two notes, Who cares, Who cares, when it enters and leaves a station; but this old train, over there, climbing the hill, tells in my ear the whole self-pitying story.

The light, like the new Diesel, is content to shriek, Who cares, Who cares.

The light seemed to lose the stealth which I had learned to associate with it. When I could see, I used to look over my shoulder in surprise, and see the sun on the small back lawn, arranging a soft picnic-spread of color. I never heard you arrive, I would say. And then, politely, If only you had told me you were coming I would have . . .

What would I have done?

It has changed now. The light clatters, rustles, leaves its volume turned up without caring for those who wish to be blind in peace. I sit—am I still without my sight?—like Erlene, in the dark.

I was blind. I am blind. A quick pinch of a word and time is adjusted, and we believe its adjustment, thinking, We have put time in its place, its pen, cell, hutch of tense, and all that remains now is to feed it, fatten it, kill it for the feast.

No, I was never blind. I would have crawled to a corner, thumped my fist against the wall (these walls which receive so much of our voice and flesh) and demanded the light. Yet in my dream I was surrounded by the atmosphere of blindness—the visits, sympathies, training schemes, meetings with the fellow-blind, societies, guide dogs, white sticks, lists of miracles; and the darkness. It all seemed like the preparations for a marriage with darkness. People's voices seemed to be charged with extra excitement when they spoke to me, as if they were to be guests at the wedding. There was almost a gaiety, a teasing quality, as if they knew that even before the ceremony the bridegroom had already claimed his share of my bed.

Then after the affair was finished, and the guests went their way, and I began my new life set aside in the margin as Blind, a terrible pity I only hope I never—, the darkness came to me without his former pretense, assurance, and we were, as fiction insists upon saying, "alone at last." But I cried. I wanted to be free. Never mind, he said, you will soon exchange the bed for a coffin, and remember that even after you die I shall stay with you, while these creatures who suddenly clasp me when their hearts stop beating shall not know the comfort of being in the arms of a friend and lover. I grew to love the darkness; it was a habit forced upon me. Before my blindness I used to welcome night with wonder and gratitude as part of the slice of variety distributed by the sun. It is so hard to believe that the sun does not live in its big double bed beyond the horizon and dutifully get up in the morning and go to sleep at night leaving us the enjoyments of darkness; that it stays always in the sky. Also, it is hard to believe that the sun does not judge us. All pretenses, proofs collapse. Why does it sit there in the sky, then, supervising, striking, training with iron the plants in the way they should grow, unless it has secret knowledge of the plan? The sun is all love and murder, judgment, the perpetual raid of conscience, paratrooping light which opens like a snow blossom in the downward drift of death. Wherever I turn—the golden cymbals of judgment, the summoning of the torturers, the inquisitors of light.

Blind, I am safe. I wonder about the warmth upon my skin, and say to myself, Out there is talk of the sun, constant chatter of light; a stray syllable arrives at my skin, embeds a meaning of warmth; well, that is so; but my darkness is one in which the sun may not spy; no one knows how far the sun has set his spies to work; they move without barriers; but in my darkness no sun may enter, for it is not the darkness resulting only from the withdrawal of light, it is a primary darkness, the first layer, the first condition of light, its foundation; it is a darkness which gives birth to a light that does not suffer the stain of human vision; a pure light resting, like a bandage, close to the deepest wound of the dark.

No, I was never blind. I would have hit with my fists and cried. I would have battled with the uncontrollable furniture, with walls and paths, striking in anger with my impotent white stick.

So I heard music. My hands crept like flies, limping, with severed wings, over the surfaces of objects. I touched. I listened. I heard music twining like a bangle around my wrist. The surface of the notes was hard, their touch was cold, menacing. And at times each note sounded in the shape of those objects which are photographed at evening, with dark shadows receding from them, or those photographs showing the last people on earth who are given disproportionately long shadows extending from diminished bodies in a mysterious violet light. I had not realized that each note of music must be accompanied by its shadow, again like the last people on earth, standing in isolation and peace when the war is over and the resting place of the blame has been decided.

Blame rests always. It is a condition of human life that blame rests, like a butterfly on a leaf. We do not care to see blame hovering about us unable to decide where to rest. No one guesses the burden of the butterfly.

The desperate shadow entered my head; the complete note. Of course, it was the sun's way of getting in!

No, I was never blind. There are such paper walls between myself and this outer world. Why should I accept less than a concrete membrane?

This terrible house, like a sea rocking. It was long ago that I came here with Edward.

26

I could never deprive myself of my senses. Oh yes, I cut off my hands, I stopped my ears, I shut my eyes; I could not smell the first smell so dear to me—the flowering currant plunging its violent uncouth waves of presence in the fresh spring air; I could not taste the frost or the green gooseberries or the half-sinking slab of creamy ice on the top of the bucket of milk.

Edward looked out at the blank silent wintry sky.

"Why did you come home here?" he asked. "There's not a sound. Even silence in this country has nothing to say."

"You must listen. There's enough talking in the air if only you listen."

But he was concerned with the sound of the generations. He chose a family whose lives (he thought) were chronicled and closed, who could not transmit to him the pain of nearness, whose distance enabled him to pluck what he needed from the long-dead fires of their daily living—the indestructible bones of love. Edward longed for the past—he is not dead, why should I use the past tense when I talk of him? Yet the lives of some people are never accommodated by the use of special tenses. Some turn to the future, others to the past, others remain in a perpetual historic present. Edward was always out of step with accepted time; it was his way of keeping alive. He chose the past as some people choose a favorite spot to live and die in—an island of palm trees, or of people, or of headstones, all connected by that rickety wartime bridge to the vast "main" where the noon is of fire and the night is of ice and survival at all times is a struggle. I have seen the desperate people of the "main" crowded at the edge of the slight swinging bridge, trying to balance their escape to the island, some plunging to the water, others fighting, making love, while the loaded sun of noon picked out with merciless light-shot the few swaying fearfully near the end of their journey. Having witnessed this desperation of people I understood why Edward should choose this one fact or family out of the past and cling to it, like a scared infant to its first source of comfort. I understood why I needed to be blind as soon as Erlene lost her power of speech: lost it or hoarded it in preparation for the judgment. But I do not think my understanding ever reached Edward, for understanding going out from one person to another has as formidable a path as the pampered youngest son who sets out to make his fortune, and stops halfway in his journey, distracted by the thought of the princess he meets and the fine castle she lives in; or bewitched by the old woman at the well; or devoured by the wild beasts of the forest. Perhaps the only way that understanding may travel from one being to another is for it to follow the conventional thread in the maze that lies between people, and risk the attack of the monster who lurks at the end of the thread.

No, he never believed that moves could be made

against loneliness by standing (or locking) two people together or in neighboring squares like pawn or king or queen. He knew that the loneliest moment in the life of a man or a woman is when both are so tangled locked wedged that the primitive nightmare strikes, Shall I ever get free, find distance, body and soul?

He was dark and shining. He wore heavily rimmed glasses because he was shortsighted.

"I cannot see you," he would say with a kind of triumph whenever he removed his glasses; as if he had satisfactorily abolished me and could now pursue his own dedicated interests. His eyes were light blue. They watered with the strain of trying to see unaided even the objects quite close to him.

"I can't see a thing," he would say, thus excusing himself from poring over the tiring prospects of his immediate environment.

So he groped for the past, and found it. Unlike most genealogists he began his research among the earliest records of the Strang family; he was not yet concerned with the living Strangs. The dead, put in their place by time, did not demand that he notice them, make love to them, provide for them. He kept their histories in little books, beautifully typed, bound, and filed. He had some idea of rescuing the human race.

So he left me, eleven years ago, to return to England, and I had heard it all before in a radio serial broadcast each morning at ten o'clock on behalf of a firm of soap manufacturers. Yet I was sad to see that soap, toothpaste, cosmetics, had replaced Death as the Leveler.

Now it is night. The centers of the poppies are deadly. Flowers in the house steal the oxygen, suck up your life, they say. I will take the withered poppies from Erlene's room and empty them on the rubbish heap outside. One cannot be too careful.

It may rain. . . .

2

She was not going to speak to anyone. She could not speak if she wanted to, because every time she opened her mouth to say something, her voice, in hiding, reminded her that there was nothing to say, and no words to say it. People usually went on talking all their lives, until just before their death, when it was said they tried to cram everything in at once, confessing. And then no one understood them. They dreamed aloud in a topped and tailed language while relations and friends leaned over them, trying to snatch their share of words that with the approach of death and silence had suddenly gone up in price. And everybody milled round in a dither, faced with unexpected treasure and desperately wanting their share. The dying were bled white; that was the expression. The living held out their pannikins for blood; or words.

Teaching people was cheating and dishonest. In the Standards, at the Middle School, when Gussy Galloway taught her, he used to say Doing Words, Describing Words, Joining Words, How When Where and Why words. But when she started to go to High School the teachers were ashamed, and added another layer—Verbs, Adjectives, Conjunctions, Adverbs, Nouns. And when the teacher talked of copulative verbs she always seemed to blush, standing there in front of the class, and putting her hand, which had no engagement or wedding ring on it, flat on certain pages of Shakespeare, and saying, Turn over the page, girls, we'll skip this scene. And then there were words which had to be looked up in the dictionary, and could not be found, not even in the supplement at the end; new words, foreign words, forbidden words, slang.

"O.K., Chief!" she said one day, and her grandfather had slapped her hard across the face.

"Slang!" he shouted. "American slang!"

Yet long before her grandfather died he used to say O.K., Chief, half-a-mo, without seeming to notice what he said, and with no one looking shocked.

She was related to the blackbeetle who sat outside on the windowsill. She watched him. He was stern and serious. He wore a black apron like an undertaker or a cobbler and he worked hard hammering and nailing. The paint on the windowsill was curled and split, and one beetle lived at one end in a little cubicle, and another beetle lived at the other end, and they seemed to get on very well without words, without even saying Hey hey to draw attention to something which they might need to tell. Did beetles tell? But what was there to tell?

I wish I were dead, Erlene thought. No I don't wish I were dead. But a big brown bird, a hawk, is flying down to pick out my insides as if I were a sheep or rabbit, and count the jewels in me, to prove everything. I think my mother would be happy if she could prove everything, if she could prove the sun and the sky, and me, and my father. I would like my mother to be happy. Other people's mothers never cry, I am sure. But mine cries. I wish she were dead, and I could speak, and not have to sit here by the window watching Uncle Blackbeetle smoothing his coffins. I keep trying to tell him that he makes them too narrow, that there will never be enough room in them. When you die, why do they grudge you a bit of extra elbowroom? Besides, you may need to take other people with you, lying side by side, but you have to lie on your back with your arms crossed and how they squeeze you in, the meanies, they pack you like a flounder alone in ice.

Uncle Blackbeetle takes no notice of me. He also mends shoes, for there is plenty of walking everywhere, walking up and down and round and round trying to decide, waiting for inspiration.

Here is my mother again, bringing poppies. "It was many and many a year ago in a kingdom by the sea . . ." "When men were all asleep the snow came flying, round the cape of a sudden came the sea, they moved in tracks of shining white, and that is why I sojourn here alone and palely loitering, though the sedge is withered from the lake and no birds sing. . . ." Sedge? The flax and rushes and flag lilies.

33

No birds sing? A bush wren, a blackbird, a sea gull following the plow.

Everything is quiet. Uncle Blackbeetle there, busy in your workshop.

There was also a snail, another distant relation, bathed in slime, fretting at his journey to the end of the world.

3

—

Edward Glace knew the attack would be successful. He had planned it the night before when he lay alone in his double bed in the hours after midnight. Every weakness of the enemy had been calculated. He had studied their supplies, transport, equipment, morale. His spies had penetrated the enemy territory many weeks ago and had returned with complete information. All was well.

It was a glorious campaign, lasting hours, and in the end the battlefield was strewn with the bodies of the enemy, the dead, and the wounded who were left to die, and the trumpets of the victorious army sounded muffled by the red haze of smoke drifting across the field. Rainwater and blood were mixed in the small pools left by the storm of two days ago; there was blood on the thistle heads and the wild flowers, and the weapons now being gathered and stored for use in the next campaign. The inescapable litter of war depressed Edward. He longed to avoid it, to remove it, to clean the battlefield—why, he wondered, did I not use one of the new Death Rays, which are cleanest of the clean, laundering death into invisibility, shrinking the monstrous dead to tiny leftovers with which one can cope, put in the palm of the hand, in an envelope, coat pocket, coin purse, wallet, paper bag; a handful of ash? What should I do? Edward wondered. What would the Strangs have done?

The excitement of the battle over, Edward grew more depressed. He found that he could not rejoice over the success of his plans. He did not even count the corpses, or send orderlies to collect the wounded. He sighed. He did not know how to award the honors. There would be no triumphal procession through the streets of the city of the kingdom with the bands playing the flags flying, cheering men and women greeting the returning forces. The warriors who returned would limp home unnoticed, in rags, and the watchdogs at the gates of the city would be set upon them to tear them to pieces, and those heroes who evaded the dogs and passed through the gates of the city of the kingdom would be greeted as strangers by their wives; none would recognize them. Besides, the battle would be forgotten, it was best forgotten, the people would say, while on the wide stretches of lawn which covered the outskirts of the city the new armies would be training, marching, practicing maneuvers, and that would be called Peace, or was it only a lizard with its tail cut off, growing a new tail, sitting on the rock of ages, in the sun?

Edward opened a can of vegetable salad, placed a slice of ham on a plate, buttered a roll, and sat down to eat. Below him on the carpet on the large piece of wallboard which was the battlefield the plastic cavalry with their antiquated lances clutched in their bright-pink plastic hands lay scattered among their stiff shining horses and cannons and the green plastic bushes arranged on the field. Edward reached down and sat one of the men upon his horse.

"Perhaps a medal for you," he said.

He glanced at the wall near the fireplace, where he had mounted his collection of medals. For some time he stared, trying to decide, but there was no decoration which would suit his hero, not among the conventional medals or the new ones which one of Edward's friends had made for him. The fact that he could find no reward for his chosen hero depressed Edward still further, and pushing aside his half-finished meal he walked over to the bed, lay down, and closed his eyes, rubbing once or twice at the few gray hairs on his balding head.

Dark hair? Dark-rimmed spectacles? For eleven years now when Vera spoke of Edward she had described him as "dark-haired with heavy-rimmed spectacles." She never doubted that she spoke the truth; such is the powerful illusion of rightness put forth by the one-party government of Memory. Erlene had caught this image of her father and when asked about him she too would reply, "dark-haired with heavy-rimmed spectacles." Who was this man, then, lying on the double bed in the room in North London, stroking his bald head with his chubby fingers, his rimless mirror-like spectacles (by a trick of the light one could see in them the reflection of three rooms—three battlefields, three filed histories of the Strang family, three of each article of furniture including three double beds with three balding men and three pairs of spectacles mirror-like rimless) lying on the table beside the bed? If he ever returned to his family how would he survive the necessary ritual of identification which must be performed even after every short absence as human beings away for five minutes, five or a million years approach one another, cross the threshold of person to person and set ringing out of the darkness the shrill commotion of alarm which must be stilled by touch, sight, sound, smell, by any of the means which identify stranger, friend, enemy. Time and change burn some people utterly. One approaches the identification of them as one approaches the scene of a disaster by fire, thankful if one recognizes a glove, a ring, two teeth as belonging to the vanished victim, as having been worn by him; things he touched, used, depended on, signaled with, and therefore part of him. Moment after moment, day after day this feverish checking is carried out as people move back and forth searching the fires of time and change. And now there is talk of destruction of the world, of human beings reduced to ashes. It is not new. It has happened often. But there has always been another human being left to complete the process of identification of his brother, to snatch wildly at a glove, a broken tooth, a wedding ring, and exclaim, I can identify him, I know him, these belong to him. And so the ashes were given a name, protection, value. When there are no human beings left on earth who will name the ashes?

The winds of love blow only in the forests of people; without them there is no more caring.

And what is it, precisely, that has vanished?

Truth may be a vast ocean within reach of all but how genuine are truths that have been drawn from the ocean, distilled, bottled, flavored, diluted, chilled, boiled, in fact adulterated with the potion of ourselves?

The Pure Truth Act requires a label to be added to each truth, stating the known percentage of adulteration.

Edward is a dark-haired man wearing dark-rimmed spectacles. Edward is a balding man wearing rimless mirror-like spectacles. Both are true, if one removes the adulteration of Time. Even in his own life Edward has tried through greed or desperation to remove Time. He is not a king or a hero but he ran as fast as his life would carry him when he realized the presence of the impure enemy, the impossibility of fighting against it, the despairing fact that he nursed it against his own left wrist, listening attentively each day to its confident heartbeats.

He got up from the bed and finished his meal, scraping the last dob of potato from the can. He gathered the soldiers in a heap, placing them in their box along with the plastic trees, farmhouses, bridges, horses, weapons. He picked up the battlefield and propped it against the wall. For a moment he wondered again whether he should award a medal to one of the soldiers leaning stiffly from the cardboard box, its face downward, as if it were vomiting and preferred to keep the box clean by vomiting on the floor of Edward's room. Which medal did the soldier deserve?

"One must praise," Edward said, "one must praise a man who vomits."

He placed the soldier in a more comfortable position by the edge of the box. Then he went to the table by the window and turned on his radio and the room was filled with the sounds of laughter and cheering and clapping—taped applause, furies of applause, but only because someone had cracked a joke at the well and the pitcher was seen to be dry, with not a drop of blood in it.

4

Again I turn from the subject of silence and consider light. I was born in the South, in an area which at that time was not served with electricity, so that when the sun went down as it early established a habit of doing, slipping beyond the banks of the muddy trout-filled river which belonged to the town and was named after it, or the town was named after the river, and what does it matter, but they lay together on the southern plain, many miles from the sea, and when the sun went down the alarm known as darkness had to be met and provided for by candles and kerosene lamps, held in the hand, preceding you when you walked along dark passages and into dark lonely rooms. My parents controlled the light and walked with it and their bodies were insignificant compared with their giant grotesque shadows striding up the wall and across the ceiling, capturing in their journey the lesser immobile shadows of furniture which nevertheless could change swiftly; everything depended upon the movement of the lamp or candle. The light was not powerful. It did not search into far corners of each room, for the rooms of the house were large and dark with cold floors smelling of pine and a borrowed smell of earth and a dusty spider-webbed smell rising from the foundations beneath the floor. Some parts of the rooms never received the glow of this artificial safeguard against night. Snap; a shot of electricity, and the guilt is searched out. No, it was not like that. People at night by candlelight and lamplight were immense shadows; it was the shadows which held the power, and everything seemed so strange, out of focus and proportion, with hands creeping along the wall, grasping more shadow, and feet deprived of their purpose, shifting and sliding, "like tea trays in the sky."

And all we had was a slight smoky defense against darkness, and in the morning or when we had settled for sleep and the lights were blown or snuffed or pinched out, the only signs of our weapon and the protection it had given us were a few blackened circles burned into the target of the ceiling.

I remember that my mother made this world of shadows more mysterious by her habit of suddenly putting her head on one side as she walked with the candle or lamp, and saying, "Hush," then quoting a snatch of verse or nursery rhyme, in particular the sinister words which set my heart thudding with terror,

> "Hark hark the dogs do bark,
> The beggars are coming to town.

Some in rags and some in bags,
and some in velvet gown."

And all up and down the gravel roads outside I could
hear the barking, and they were no dogs which I knew
or had seen by daylight, not collies docilely at heel or
briskly setting the sheep in order or bringing home the
cows at milking time, but strange menacing dogs, taller
than myself, attacking the lonely huddle of beggars who
had no house to go to, no bed to sleep in or fire to warm
them, but had to pass through a different town each
night, secretively, on their lonely journey, trying at all
costs to avoid the dogs which lay in wait for them, to
tear them to pieces because they did not belong in the
town, they were beggars, and some were in rags, and
some in bags and velvet gown. Often I heard or seemed
to hear an urgent scuffling and wild barking outside our
house, then a repeated scraping and knocking, and I
would glance at my mother, inquiring, not speaking,
Shall I let them in? I hoped that she would say No,
never!, for I was afraid of them, and surely our house
had no place fit for beggars, surely they were difficult
people to fit anywhere, for none of their measurements
were like ours! Yet I was disappointed and unhappy
when after seeming to listen for a moment to the frantic
knocking, my mother yet made no mention of it, as if she

43

had never heard it. Everyone pretended not to hear it. Perhaps it was bad manners to talk of it or seem aware of it. Soon, however, the knocking would cease, there would be a sound of retreating footsteps, and the beggars would be gone on their way, chased by the dogs, to the next house, Mrs. Turner's, whose hedge was high and whose lawn was smooth and bright green. And the next morning the streets would be empty of beggars and of giant dogs, with no scrap of rag, bag, or velvet gown lying on the footpath or in the gutter. It was evident that no one in the town had given food or shelter to the beggars, and that even now, in the morning sunshine, they were already on their way, crossing the plains to reach the next town by nightfall. It had not been fair of them or of the dogs to frighten us in the night. I was relieved that they had gone taking their hunger and misery with them.

We had porridge for breakfast, cooked in an iron pot, and stirred with the spurtle which hung on the hook by the stove. We drank big overflowing cups of milk. The sun shone. The lamps and candles were put away. Darkness and the shadows and the beggars would never come again.

On the east coast, in the South, there was a beach, Waipapa, with its own lighthouse. How strange to have a special house for light! But the sea, we learned, could not be relied upon, it was full of whims and treacheries and the bones of dead men, and it was the purpose of the lighthouse to prevent the death of men by warning the ships of dangerous currents or rocks. So many constructions, arrangements, ideas, ways of behaving, were directed to prevent the death of men, of people. People were valuable, though not, of course, if they were beggars, and then the dogs could take care of them in the night. Year after year so many lives were saved by the use of the lighthouse and the powerful beacon restlessly turning and flashing in the dark, controlled and guarded by the Keeper who lived alone in the tower and was supplied with food, fuel, medicine, by a ship whose journey round the coast was often a perilous one: in winter the ship was delayed and for weeks the Keeper received no supplies or letters and talked to no one. His only companion was the light, his only message the distant signals flashed by passing ships; yet locked with his beacon in the stone tower and deprived of most of the amenities of civilization, he remained, they said, one of the happiest men alive. So they said. We played and picnicked in the sand dunes and listened to the seabirds crying, and we stared at the sleeping lighthouse that waited only for the night, to set its beacon revolving and flashing, to save men from death; for during the day the light was no match for the sun, which nevertheless put

45

forth no signals or warnings but allowed men to die; the sun not gesturing with dismay but spreading a silver tinsel on the water as if to say Death is a cheap occasion, a makeshift festival arranged for the benefit of human commerce, with the purchase and exchange of tasteless signed cards of darkness and light and festoons of false glitter tangled between sea and sky. It was terrible that the sun should admit its lack of sympathy with drowning men, should so insistently place the responsibility for pity upon the men themselves—sailing or drowning or walking in smart suits along the streets of the city, or fleeing at night in rags and tags and velvet gown from the savage dogs set upon them by men. The sun rolls over in the sky. The light falls heavily as responsibility. The shoulders of men are bowed under the weight of the light which for all its lack of pity is yet an ally in man's war against death.

And what of the keeper alone for so long with Light?

I was only little, just so high, and I did not consider much about the sun except its burning and sliding down the wet leaves when the rain had stopped, and its quality of morning. I played on the beach among the sand dunes, and listened to the seabirds crying, and then one day I saw a small boat struggling against the waves, being steered from the lighthouse, and as it came nearer I saw that one of the three men in it was waving his arms and

screaming while the others tried to cope with him. It was
the lighthouse keeper marooned for too long with Light.
He had gone mad. The wind was filled with sand, stinging and hot, and the seabirds wheeled and cried. The
lonely posturing figure was set down on the beach. He
trod the sand as if he believed it might have been water.
He tried to reenter the water, to run and plunge in.
Then, surrendering because he was being held so tightly
by his companions, he stopped the wild moving of his
limbs and instead let out a high-pitched scream, like a
seabird. He had changed to a seabird.

I did not understand. We were picnicking. We were
going to have tomatoes—in sandwiches, and whole with
the seeds spitting in our eyes. No one mentioned the
lighthouse keeper. My mother turned her face away, as
if the beggars had knocked on her door. My father said
sharply to me, "Don't stare at what doesn't concern
you!"

So that I missed seeing whether the lighthouse keeper
really changed to a bird, flying round and round under
the sun, or whether they took him away along the sand
to the town where they locked him safely in another
tower, as they lock people who have been alone too long
with light.

Do you know that they take people from tower to
tower, up and down up and down the spiral stair?

I am oppressed by the gloom of light, by the attempt to copy its gloom in neon, sodium, putting a ring round the world in a way which the smudged sputtering thumbprint of candle or kerosene flame could never manage, grasped in the trembling hand of people standing strange in one place, in one house, with the beggars pleading outside and the dogs barking. The world is plunged too suddenly into light. Now no crime escapes detection—see how people's thoughts are deprived of shadow, how the insignificant and remarkable stand in equal brilliance under the sodium light, without the shame of a puny telltale shadow or the triumph of a world-blotting shade which cancels the very shape which it claims to serve, to lay a path for, cool shade beneath immense thought.

Shade and silence.

Erlene is in bed now, sleeping. The doctors have said that one morning she may wake and find that she can speak again, that I must not appear astonished or overjoyed (how little they realize my secret desires) but must continue whatever I happen to be doing as if her speech were an everyday fact. I have written to Edward telling him of her loss of speech. I addressed the letter carefully and posted it but it was returned with the words on the envelope *Not Known At This Address*. Yet he *is* known there, he *lives* there. I shall write another letter. I believe that each person's life contains one message which never reaches its destination. I deceive myself by thinking that I can repeat the message. This compulsory stopping of communication is a dismal reminder of our ultimate dependence upon silence, of the fact that in the end there is really nothing to say, that silence is our true companion and partner and lover. In spite of Edward's or any man's concern with the generations (searching, groveling for, polishing, setting, attaching bead after bead to the supposedly charmed necklace worn by Procreation), all true begetting is from silence, without history or time or place. Somerset House, The British Museum, the basement of the London Library do not contain the more important records of the generations of silence.

Perhaps it is no use anymore, this throwing of dice inside our hollow skulls and admiring the pretty pattern of sixes, as if we had contrived and controlled them. One must go deep, deeper than the silence of one person near or far in blood; the enemy is so close, there is so much confusion, so many layers of light, and all day and night now in the secret gloom we keep stopping to listen, to incline our head, and say

"Hark Hark the dogs do bark,
the beggars are coming to town,

> some in rags and some in bags,
> and some in velvet gown."

How soon shall we learn enough to be able to open the door to them without putting ourselves in more grave danger? How soon shall we learn to break the silence and speak to them?

5

―

Sometimes as she sat alone by the window she would take a book from the many on her shelves and begin to read. When she got up from her chair and walked across to the bookshelf she was always surprised to find that she could walk, that she was not crippled or paralyzed and that her chair, the old armchair which her grandfather had used, and perhaps his grandfather before him, was a simple ordinary chair, not fussed and guiltily explaining itself and her with wheels, levers, brakes, as if to say, This is the secret of moving, moving is not in your body anymore Erlene.

She used to read poetry, all the poems she had once read at school with the other girls there sitting in their desks, and the teacher in her black gown standing in front of the class, up on the platform, for their classroom had been used as an assembly hall, and still contained the Honors Board where each year in the long summer holidays when there was no one around to peer and pry, the latest names were added in gold lettering which did not seem quite dry even when the girls returned to school, as if, had they rubbed their sleeves against the name, it would have been obliterated, or the letters would have curled up and dropped from the wall as no name, nothing but shavings of gold paint. And that showed how easily words could be torn, distorted, made unrecognizable, or removed altogether. So many names were honored on the School List. Soon there would be no room for them as the list overflowed into column after column—prefects, heads of school, the dux for each year, the tennis, swimming champion, University Honors . . . they would have to find some method of choosing the most honored from among the already chosen, and then again choosing from the chosen of the chosen, until perhaps there would be only one name left on the Honors Board, and even that name, when the arguments and jealousies and further suggestions made themselves known, would ultimately be removed, and there would be nothing but a blank wall.

That would be neat, Erlene said to herself, thinking of it.

Every year they had given her high marks for neatness, for ruling lines and drawing circles, and writing "Conclusion" at the end of each experiment. Given, To Prove, Construction, Proof, Conclusion.

That was Geometry. There were speech lessons too, with choral speaking in charge of Miss Walters who had a face like a Jersey cow and who, when the class was reciting, would move her arms back and forth in rhythm, like sails in the wind. She wore brown clothes, and blouses with tucks in front, smocked over her bosom.

Her hair was going gray, and when she swallowed her throat drooped suddenly, and bulged, as if she chewed a cud.

"Bright is the ring of words when the right man rings them," she would chant, reefing and striking sail. And,

> "A song of enchantment I sang me there
> in a green green wood by waters fair."

She lived with her mother on the South Hill, and her sister worked in the town library. Sometimes, to the disgust of the class, Miss Walters asked them to recite a poem which they had learned years ago in the Infant Room and which belonged among clapping games, beads, paper cutouts, and had no place with High School girls. It was called "Someone," and began,

> Someone came knocking at my wee small door,
> Someone came knocking, I'm sure, sure, sure,
> I listened, I opened, I looked to left and right,
> and nought there was a-stirring in the still dark night

and ended with the line, "And no one came knocking at my wee small door," which Miss Walters spoke sadly, turning sometimes to stare at the schoolroom door, as if she expected a visitor.

Miss Walters cycled to school every morning, and

sharp at half-past eight she crossed the railway line at the foot of the hill, near the post office, and sharp at twenty-five to nine she passed the Queen's Hotel, and sharp at twenty to nine she passed Cater's Garage, and at a quarter to nine she turned the corner into the street by the High School gates. Miss Walters was so sharp!

Sharp and lonely, and her mother was deaf, they said, and had to be shouted at.

And Erlene was dumb. She hadn't always been unable to speak, oh no, she had been able to say A song of enchantment I sang me there, and Bright is the ring of words when the right man rings them, and later, in the higher classes,

> Round the cape of a sudden came the sea,
> and the sun looked over the mountain's rim. . . .

and

> The sea is calm to-night.
> The tide is full, the moon lies fair
> Upon the straits; . . .

with the ending,

> Ah, love, let us be true
> To one another! for the world, which seems

54

To lie before us like a land of dreams,
So various, so beautiful, so new,
Hath really neither joy, nor love, nor light,
Nor certitude, nor peace, nor help for pain; . . .

which caused Miss Walters to explain that Matthew
Arnold had suffered attacks of despair at the state of the
world and the sufferings of man.

"What nonsense, really," Miss Walters would say, gazing round the classroom and smiling brightly. "Why the
world is full of hope and joy! You must remember, girls,
that when poets write in this way it is usually because
they are ill or overstrained; the despair is a part of their
illness."

Then, at the end of the lesson, Miss Walters, who was
also the tennis coach, would exclaim in a voice full of
hope at the variety, beauty and newness of the world,
"Girls, tennis tonight is on the top court, near the School
House. Four-fifteen sharp."

Sharp.

Sharp and lonely.

Her books were on three shelves which her grandfather built a year before he died. She had been afraid of
her grandfather because neither he nor the house seemed
to fit in with her or her mother's life. He was ugly, like
a goblin, with no top teeth and blackened bottom ones,
and when he walked his knees seemed to bend giving him

the appearance of dancing and sometimes of suddenly having to submit to a pain inside him, like the gripes, as if he had been eating green gooseberries. When he walked his hands were never still but kept grasping at objects in his path, either to reassure himself of their presence, or to lay claim to them, the most significant claim of all, by touching them with a part of his body; or he may have been using the objects as milestones to guide him, for he was getting old—he was over seventy—and when you are old the space you live in expands, to fool you, to prepare you for the time when you are still, traveling nowhere, inside your own worldwide coffin.

Her grandfather lived quite apart from herself and her mother. He seemed to regard her mother with suspicion, as if in traveling overseas and returning with a child and a husband she had brought a nameless infection into the house. Therefore her grandfather kept to himself, pottering about the house and the grounds, obstinately trying every year, as he had done for most of his married life, to grow cucumbers. He had never managed to grow cucumbers. He grew pumpkins, marrows, beans, most other vegetables, and prize chrysanthemums, but not cucumbers.

Erlene could remember, from a long time ago, her grandfather standing with her father by the flower garden outside the front-bedroom window, and her grandfather with a look of anger on his face, saying the names of the flowers, and looking even angrier when her father said something, she could not hear what it was, and pointed to one of the flowers. Her father was wearing a pair of baggy pants which, he kept saying, he had bought in Arabia. He also kept saying how warm the pants were in winter, and how cool in summer.

"They must be handy," her grandfather had said without interest, speaking almost as he spoke when he was annoyed.

But one day when Erlene was playing marrieds by herself in the front bedroom, sitting on the floor by the bed, scolding her husband for staying late at the library, the door opened and her grandfather walked in and picked up the Arabian pants hanging over the back of the chair. He touched them, making in an undertone the exclamation which he used when he wanted to admire.

"By Jove. By Jove!"

The expression on his face told not that he wished for a pair of Arabian pants to keep him warm in winter and cool in summer, but that he longed to go to Arabia. Hiding under the bed, growing tired of playing marrieds, Erlene crept out to her grandfather and took him by the arm, pleading, "Take me too!"

Her grandfather spoke in a loud voice.

"Take you where?"

"That place where my father bought them."

Erlene pointed to the baggy pants.

"Arabia?"

"Yes, Arabia."

"What!" her grandfather roared suddenly. "You stay in your own country and don't go gallivanting round the world!"

Frightened, Erlene ran and hid under the bed, and played marrieds again, but it was all right because her husband was home from the library, and they had a wonderful time together all evening, feasting, sitting opposite each other with silver knives and forks and gold plates and cups eating pineapples until they were full.

She could choose any book she liked. She was grateful for that. The most frightening book was an old dictionary with thin pages packed with words, each page covered with tiny letters like the black fly dung on the kitchen window. There was also a book about Arabia, and a poem which began,

> Far are the shades of Arabia
> where the princes ride at noon.

But Erlene was old enough to know that it was not like that anymore, it had never been like that, there was all disease and desert and fighting and hunger. Yet perhaps some day, even now, she would go to Arabia, even if she was not able to speak.

When her father went back to England, years ago,

he had not taken the Arabian pants. At first her mother and her grandfather forgot about them, and they hung on the hook in the passage beside the "Storm at Sea," and then one day her mother washed the pants and when she was bringing them in from the clothesline her grandfather reached out to touch them, saying, "Let me see again, yes, they would do for winter and summer, the Arabians know what they're about."

Her mother put the pants away in a drawer, and then after a few years when she was cleaning the room and examining those souvenirs which had not yet been destroyed, she took the pants, tore them in half, used one half for a duster and threw the other half in a corner of the washhouse upon a pile of old rags and papers. And then one winter evening a black-and-white stray tabby with a sore nose and scratched ears came in out of the cold of the surrounding paddocks where it lived with other strays in hedges and ditches and under the gum trees and the matagouris, and lay down in the corner of the washhouse on the now moth-eaten Arabian pants, and had four black-and-white kittens.

Uncle Blackbeetle took off his apron and leaned forward,

"Tell me all about it, Erlene," he said.

6

———

When people learned from Edward, as they did sooner or later for he saw no reason to conceal the fact, that he had not seen his family for eleven years but that he considered himself a married man, a responsible father, most were inclined to express some feeling of astonishment, as when an apparently harmless human being (for people will forever consider naïvely that a harmless human being exists) is found out in murder. Edward's appearance, particularly his spectacles (though people might have experienced alarm if they gazed into his eyes and saw themselves reflected three times) gave him a conventional air of mildness which caused anyone who tried to sum up his character at first glance to make that strange rather sinister remark which really implies inhuman tolerance of disease and death—"He would not hurt a fly."

Edward had his obsessions; they were his property; he was concerned that the human race should continue, that the generations should follow each other like the flowers which open at morning,

> and fill the air with an innumerable dance
> yet all in order sweet and lovely.

60

He saw his method of abandoning his own family and devoting his life to the study of the remote Strangs (though in fact they were close now; he had reached the living generation) as no worse and certainly less liable to produce disaster than the habits of other people whose concern for the preservation of the human race led them to nurse bombs on their lap, feeding them with love and care on strained ideals and principles from which the "goodness" had been boiled away.

Edward lived, as he wished to fight with his plastic armies, by remote control. Also he liked power; he liked to be able to make the awards now, to judge *personally*. The Strangs haunted him. They persisted about him, their voices echoing, whispering. They were an ordinary family—he had been particular about tracing the lineage of an "ordinary family" because he was aware that families, so described, share the common nightmare, put poison in one another's food, bed, and brain, and make love with the taste of death in their mouths, breathing it in their partner's face or trying to get rid of it by first swallowing little green tablets colored like silkworm dung. An ordinary family, in the chain gang of the human race, linked in the ordinary way with doom.

Knowing the story of Edward's life and hearing his frequent cynical remarks one would not have guessed his deep concern and care for humanity. He wanted only to fulfill a small ambition, to make a complete beautiful chronicle of one family which had persisted over the centuries in spite of war, disease, and other catastrophes which have visited mankind. To Edward the important fact of each war, plague, earthquake, famine, was not the number killed but the realization that at one moment during the disaster two people were giving expression of their love for each other, were lying nakedly giving and receiving, in spite of deceits disgusts errors calamitous misunderstandings, with that ultimate generosity and gratitude which create in the human mind among tenements of despair enough believing-space and praising-space for a God.

With such an ideal before him, with such a vision of generations of lovers, Edward found his own love-making perfunctory and disappointing, a disaster of the blood which took toll of his strength and his temper while promising so much. He had made love to the woman who came four evenings a week to type and file his genealogical notes. It had not been satisfactory. Her guilt depressed him.

"What would the Strangs think?" she asked, in the same way that people call on their parents, What would your father, your mother say? What would your wife say? or, God is looking, spying from the sky with his little eye!

Edward was surprised to find that it mattered to him

what the Strangs would think, that now he had discovered the living generation, and had planned the letters he would write to arrange meetings with the family, he was continually wondering, What will they think of me? What will the Strangs think? Was his project any use as an effort to rescue the human race? Surely a man could not spend so many years, giving up his wife and family, to work at a task which was wasteful and bad and useless! Yet people do, he told himself, people even spend eighty or ninety years *living*.

The real reason, Edward said to himself, is the principle of the matter. It is best to make sure.

He rubbed his eyes, which only that morning had begun to water continually, so that he found it hard to see, and was forced to keep brushing away the watery substance; at the same time he dismissed the fantastic idea that he was weeping. Tears for whom? Why?

He did not often listen to music, although he liked chamber music because it reached a thin rung of the mind where the heavy-footed could not venture, at least not without wearing a safety harness. But as he sat now on one of the small hard chairs arranged in rows before the table where the doctor and nurse were examining each patient, he thought he would choose statistics rather than the music which emerged from somewhere in the wall.

"It's Light and Bright," explained the patient sitting

next to him. "I come here often for my eyes, and it's Light and Bright. There's also cocktail and Latin American."

"How interesting," Edward said, glancing enviously at his companion, whose right eye was covered in bandages.

"Quite interesting. They're busy, aren't they?"

The man nodded.

The tunes continued. Edward wondered, Now what makes the authorities suppose that music more than statistics will put us at our ease. They could avoid the births deaths and other depressing statistics, and pipe all day from somewhere in the wall the sort of information which magazines use to fill in space—the number of miles of nylon stockings sold each year, or the number of miles walked by the average housewife; if this proves too depressing they could turn to the insect world—as people do, considering the ants.

Edward rubbed a fresh discharge of watery substance from his eyes. "It's only the principle," he told himself. "Just to find out if anything's wrong with my sight."

He was surrounded by rows of people, some of whom had been waiting all morning and most of whom had bandaged eyes. There was subdued conversation giving details of the accident, the illness, the prognosis, all in a soft swirl of animated statistics. Edward was annoyed to discover that he wished his eyes were bandaged. The other patients seemed to glance at him suspiciously because his eyes were not bandaged. They evidently thought he was a fraud. He felt that he should not have made an appointment; there was nothing the matter with his eyes; they kept watering, making unasked-for tears; and that was nothing; it was not blindness anyway.

At last Edward's turn came for examination. He was humiliated at once.

"How did you get here?" the doctor asked. "There's nothing wrong with your eyes. All you need is a new prescription for your glasses."

The doctor looked resentfully at Edward's eyes, as if he rather wished they had been diseased. Edward wished the same. The doctor felt cheated. Edward felt cheated also. He longed to be swathed in bandages, to forget about the preservation of the human race, the Strangs, the Bomb, only to be swathed in bandages and be accepted among the people with sore eyes, and have the doctor look at him with a quickening of interest and approval, even of admiration.

Edward was ashamed of his feelings.

"Next please," the doctor said coldly, directing Edward to the insignificant corner cubicle reserved for people who were merely changing the prescription of their glasses. Edward pulled aside the curtain and went in. It was like one of those tiny places in chain stores where you pay half a crown and pose and your photograph is taken and when it is developed, five minutes later, it shows you with a red shining face and glazed eyes as if you were living in the shadow of a fire of goodness and imbecility.

When Edward returned from the hospital he found two letters waiting for him. One was from a member of the Strang family. He put it aside. The other was from Vera. He opened it, and read that Erlene had lost her power of speech, and that it seemed unlikely that she would ever talk again.

7

I deceive myself; I cheat. I grant myself blindness, accepting it as a deserved gift. I spend so much time writing here while my only daughter sits lonely and silent by her window (in the sun, though; the sun shines in there at morning, it rises over the sea, casting a cool silver glow on the water, like the twinkling of fishes of light caught in the new net of morning). This room, littered now with the white sticks of my trade—my advertisement to myself of my blindness and my peril in the traffic which flows in my mind—is the same room where I lived from late childhood before I left to go to University and later to make that journey overseas at the whim and expense of Aunt Lena, who died in a bedroom where the wallpaper was patterned with outsize roses and a dark-blue china water jug stood on the washstand. I merely state the spatial conditions of her death—east, north, south, west, the roses; southeast, the water jug topped with soap scum.

Aunt Lena left me eight hundred pounds to be used solely for a "journey overseas," for like so many of the dead she made certain of transferring her wishes and the fulfillment of them to the living. Lying in the dark, wet, and cold of one's coffin, with the burden of earth, acceptance, death, propriety, and public health making it impossible for one to escape, one may perhaps think with satisfaction of the conditions one has imposed upon the living. Aunt Lena's long-standing wish was to go "overseas" to "trace" her grandfather's family. Her death and the outsize roses on the wallpaper and the half-filled water jug, and her need to make pilgrimage to an old country churchyard and tear (furiously, with claws) the grass and moss from the gravestone of a stranger, all led to my meeting with Edward, my marriage, and the birth of Erlene.

Edward and I were fleet enough in the hemispheres.

"We have seven-leagued boots now," he said. "But that does not mean that we are giants. Even when the human race stands at its tallest there will always be headroom, enough for the demons to fly back and forth and clouds to cluster like soft white maggots about the sun."

I caught his concern for humanity. He talked of the Bomb, of soft white ash like talcum powder clogging the pores of the earth—like a deodorant, though not like lilies or jasmine, only the smell of nothing removing without trace the smell of humanity, all its pools of blood, sweat, tears, semen, milk; a mere dusting of talcum powder; and trees with white hair; and a blue flame in the valleys; and night falling as usual with the stars coming out in their correct places and shining, and frost visiting, and the night wind mistaking the ruins for trees and crying there through hollows and caverns; and the darkness; and no one to say the sun does not care; and in the morning, sunrise, or rain, and a well-kept rainbow perfect in the sky.

"I don't know," Edward said, arranging the Strangs like an army.

Erlene was born. We returned to New Zealand. Edward left to pursue his circular interests. The day he left, Erlene was wearing those cream satin ballet shoes which cripple the feet under pretense of teaching them how to dance.

I remember that I too was a schoolgirl when we came to live in this house. After we moved from the little inland town that was named after the river or the river was named after the town, we lived in a house here near the main street, but we were given notice, and I was old enough to join the search up hill and down dale studying To Let and For Sale placards, in imagination living in each of the empty windowless houses, visiting and inspecting them as one visits a grave, with flowers in our hands, for we could never resist picking the roses and poppies and pansies from the overgrown gardens. And then there were frightening interviews when our mother or father called on the estate agents and solicitors, with their offices in the Town Hall Chambers; and people kept shaking their heads and saying No, No. I remember my mother remarking in her dignified way, "I might be dressed in rags but I am no criminal. If you give us time we will pay. Only give us time."

When my mother spoke the last phrase it was my turn to feel ashamed, for there was no dignity in her saying it; she was pleading. Give us time. How strange! It is the same phrase which Edward began muttering in his sleep, after the Strangs took over his mind and someone planted the Bomb along the borders of his care!

It seemed in those days when we wandered the streets in search of a house that we would never find anywhere to live. I consoled myself— Well, I knew a little house, a spider's house in a dock leaf where I could make my home without paying and with inconvenience to no one. It had white curtains and rust-colored walls with gold and orange splashes down them; my own little house. Would the grown-ups understand if I quietly packed my things and tiptoed out the front door at midnight when the moon was shining on the stone doorstep?

At last we found this house. We bought it cheaply because no one else wanted it, there were no conveniences, and the kitchen floor was earth, with the rats living there, and the mice in the bedrooms, and outside there was a washhouse with a copper and a rusty bath; but we bought the house, and paid for it, and repaired it, putting a new floor in the kitchen and a bath in the new bathroom, and a lavatory which was not a rusty kerosene tin set in a deep hole by the dunny roses. Wild people had lived in the house before us; wild mad people; tramps; prostitutes; people who had been in prison for the kind of crimes which are found out and therefore punished. I learned that to carry out this punishment the authorities built small rooms with barred windows; there was such a place down Severn Street not far from our new home. We passed it as we passed the morgue, with dread and delight, hoping at the morgue to catch a glimpse of death, not the kind of death which visits homes and is occasion for black ties, mournful speech, brisk (though sober, except for Uncle Harry who was drunk and shouted at the funeral Good riddance, Be seeing you!) comings and goings, arranging of cards and letters and wreaths, but death tidied up, made official, with a model corpse who was related to nobody; in the same way we hoped to see peering from the small barred window of the prison in Severn Street a paragon of a criminal, not a man or woman or any human being who was related to anybody, no one who had been born and had gone to school and got married, who got up in the morning and had breakfast, went shopping, went to the lavatory, went to sleep, but just a Criminal; peering sad and penitent through the barred window onto Severn Street.

71

"Perhaps dancing will rescue humanity," Edward said.

It is so long since I have seen him. I do not like to confess that the image of him—dark, with glossy hair and dark-rimmed spectacles—has blurred and faded until I find it hard to believe in its truth—or should I say in *my* truth. It was soon after he left that I nursed my father in his last illness, and although I say his "last" illness, he had not been ill before, but the word "last" gives a dignity and meaning to the prolonged enfeeblement which by itself is without dignity but which placed so close to the time of death becomes an affair of grand irony and beauty—even in the watering eyes, running nose, the splashes of excrement, the marvelous choice which the mind seems to exercise in cutting off the means of communication in preparation for the final silence; now the sense of smell is lost, now the hearing "goes" and a placid stupid expression appears on the invalid's face as we talk to him—he is giving us his final opinion of the value of human speech; an obstinate loss of sight—No, I cannot see, why should I want to see, in all this dark; the infuriating infantile preoccupation with making senseless movements, waving the arms, the legs, as if he is learning once again the mechanics of walking in a sudden attempt to express his utter disbelief in the prospect of his death, to show his determination to begin life again and again; the slow, domestic, inti-

72

mate decline; the last days marked, like the first, with feeding and changing, and inviting a minister from the church to dangle pretty baubles of promise, such gay colors, washable, with no arsenic in the paint, waved back and forth in front of the tired pleading eyes.

My father was not really ill, only suffering a slow diminishing of life which seemed to prescribe areas of occupation for him, and set him down there, directing him from one to the other as he came nearer the time to die. First there was the small backyard where my father seemed content to stay pottering in the sunlight, calling out to the magpies when they crowded the roof of the old dunny, saying Tweet Tweet to the friendly fantail which he now insisted, though formerly he used to mock at the idea, was the same fantail which my mother had petted, calling it to the kitchen window and feeding it with crumbs and pieces of dripping, in spite of the fact that many generations of fantails had lived since my mother's death.

No one expressed surprise when my father no longer pottered about in the yard but sat all day in the armchair which we moved out in the yard in the daytime and carried in at night; or when he stayed inside, sitting in the armchair by the stove and no longer caring to sun himself, but looking out of the window at the second-hand daylight, remarking without his former passion on the sun and the weather and the temperature. He was no longer involved with "outside." He did not even care to indulge in his favorite pastime of forecasting the weather; tomorrow did not seem to matter. It was only a few yards, then, from his chair to the bedroom, and the new phase of life in bed where he weakened quickly now, tormented by trivial things like patterns on the wall and an owl rustling in the tree outside, an owl or an opossum.

"I get no rest," he complained. "Owls and opossums all night."

He was grateful for the electric blanket which I bought him with part of Edward's generous allowance. He was suspicious at first.

"Sleep on that, and be electrocuted? No fear!"

Later, when I had used it for myself and for Erlene and he realized that neither of us had been electrocuted, he allowed me to put it in his bed, provided he supervised the switching on and off.

"It's dandy, it's warm," he said the next morning, stroking the blanket.

"My word, it's dandy!"

The frosts were bitter; the pipes froze. My father would stroke the electric blanket, and smooth it, and try to read the writing on the label in the top left-hand corner, as if it were a personal message for him. He asked to see the instruction booklet. He could not quite believe the warmth which seemed to him to be a special

74

gift from the blanket itself, a disinterested act of kindness.

"My word," he would repeat. "It's dandy, just dandy!"

But he used it for only one winter. He died the following June after a week of heavy rain that swirled as mist about the hilltops and the gum plantation up the road, near the Williams' farm, though old Mr. Williams was dead now and the herd had been sold, and the boy Williams had gone to America with an agricultural scholarship. My father had not been on speaking terms with the Williamses ever since he had driven the cow up the road to Williams' bull and been turned away by old Mr. Williams, who said he was particular which cows were serviced by his bull, and did our cow have a test certificate?

"It's a reflection on us," my father had said, when he returned with the bellowing unsatisfied cow.

There was also a bother, and exchange of abuse, when Mr. Williams claimed that the plants on our property were having what he called "a bad effect" on his bees and their honey.

"I don't ask the bees to come here. Nobody invites them," my father said. "As a matter of fact, they're trespassing."

But in the long summer days of January and February our orchard and paddock and garden were filled with bees. I remember studying one or two in order to find a mark that would distinguish them as belonging to Mr. Williams. They all seemed hungry, happy, and healthy enough in their buzzing—oh the days were hot, and the noise of bees filled the air that was dusty with pollen and sun haze, and there were tiny black flies stuck to one another crowded by the creek and a creek stink rising from the deep pool under the willow tree where a wheat sack of new kittens had been drowned, and their tiny terrible struggling had shot like an electric current through the confusion of muddy water and up the arm of the person who had tied the stone around the mouth of the sack and thrust it into the water; and the culprit had not been able to brush away the current; it penetrated her body and made her heart beat with fear and pity.

I was the culprit.

The winter that my father died there were no pools or shallows in the creek that surrounds our house; there was only a foaming river which surged above the bridge and prevented us from leaving the hillock on which this house is built. It rained and rained. The windows streamed continually like the windows of a railway carriage when the train is traveling faster and faster against a storm. But our house was not moving. I was surprised to find that our house was not moving. My father was in bed, in the room next to the kitchen. From his bed he could look down the path onto the flat and see the creek.

"We're cut off," he moaned. "I knew we'd be cut off."

I tried to reassure him, telling him that it would not be for long, it was never for long, didn't he remember that last time it had rained in this way and the creek stayed only two days in flood?

"We never had rain like this before," my father said. He was weeping and plucking at the bedclothes with hands that had got so thin they seemed like hands grafted from the dead, they were surely not the hands that had built the old kitchen table and the bookshelves for Erlene and conducted a feud with cucumbers!

"We haven't paid for the electric blanket. Ten to one they'll be asking for the money now, when we're cut off. I always knew we'd be cut off. Didn't I say? Didn't I?"

I did not try to tell him that the electric blanket had been paid for long ago.

He closed his eyes.

"What's the use if you're cut off?"

Then he licked his lips suddenly and greedily.

"What about food?"

I told him that the creek would be at its normal level in a day or two, that in the meantime we had no need to go shopping or visiting, that Erlene was probably enjoying the excitement of being surrounded by water and not being able to go to school, that there were plenty of supplies in the house until the Star Stores delivered our order at the weekend. My father was suspicious.

"What supplies? How do you know what we'll need, now we're cut off? And there's no sandsoap in the house either."

He slept then, his face suddenly gray as if any blood remaining in his cheeks had rushed elsewhere in his body in response to an alarm, an emergency.

In the morning he was dead, the rain had stopped, and the creek was halfway to its normal level. On my way across the bridge to fetch a neighbor—for what is death without neighbors? this I learned from my mother—I noticed just below the tidemark, swept onto the crushed soaking yellow-stained grass of the bank, the telltale sack, which had been washed up in the flood. It was rotted, hanging in threads; the stone was still tied around it; it seemed to be empty. I wondered if the story were true that cats always escape from drowning; then I knew it was false as the belief and hope that people, weighed down by life, with the stone cruelly in its place, can escape from the darkness of the surrounding flood.

8

When Uncle Blackbeetle took off his apron and set aside his cutting cleaning and polishing tools, she noticed that his skin was brown and shining, his eyes were large and black, overhanging his face like streetlamps, and there were dark tracks up and down his face which, lit by his eyes, became caverns, ravines flowing with underground rivers. Without his apron he was a brown beetle, brown as a ripe acorn. If the sun burns him, she thought, he will snap in two and put forth cream and green shoots; he will expand in the sun and spill all his cargo. How hard he works! She was afraid that he might ask her age, because she would not be able to tell him, and she felt ashamed of not knowing her age, because once you have lost your place, your special hanger in the dark coat cupboard that fills the world of time, then there is nowhere for you to go to keep clean and free from dust and the moth grubs which chew your face in the dark and spit out the wishbones behind your eyes. Uncle Blackbeetle did not ask her age; but that was no help; she still did not know it. Someone had whipped away the cozy number of years and left her alone and strange and stared at, like something freakish disclosed by the conjurer who deftly removes the concealing sheet of silk.

For a long time she stared at Uncle Blackbeetle, and he stared at her, then she found to her surprise that she could talk to him.

"Why do you keep making those little coffins on the windowsill?" she asked.

"It is my trade," he said. "I work for the bean family, and every day there are deaths among the beans, mostly from thirst. They shrivel and die, they go blind in their one black eye, and I put them in one of these tiny coffins. Beans, you know, are beautifully shaped, like a new church, like modern architecture, like a planned city—I know these through my cousins."

"You have relations then? Mothers and fathers and sisters and brothers; aunts, uncles? Do you keep in touch?"

"Miraculously so, with communication at all points of the earth."

"Letters?"

"Letters."

"What language do you write in?"

"Language?"

"I mean which set of words do you use? There is such a wide choice. Would you like to borrow my dictionary?"

"I had a cousin once who lived in your dictionary, inside the binding, and there was a tiny hole which he used for a door, and it led out between *trichotomy* and *trick*. Now what do you think of that? It was only a few minutes walk to *trigger*, then over the page to *trinity*, *trinket* and *trional*, and there my cousin used to fall asleep. He was quite an ignorant cousin. He believed that he was stopping at railway stations each time he arrived at a word, and what did he do then but look around expecting to be provided with refreshment; at each word, mind you; sometimes he found it, other times he didn't, and he died without knowing the difference between words and railway stations. I myself passed by your dictionary one day but I did not go in. I am a busy beetle. Besides, dictionaries are dangerous."

Erlene grew afraid of Uncle Blackbeetle then. He was staring at her with his eyes burning bright.

He smiled strangely.

"Would you like me to put on a white coat and come here to visit you? And would you like to talk to me, using words?"

"But I've been using words."

"No you haven't. You haven't been speaking at all. Shall I put on a white coat and a clean smile for you?"

"Not a white coat," Erlene answered. "Put on your black apron. I will sew a monogram on it for you, using a transfer. I learned to sew monograms in the Primary School. Monograms are proof that you belong somewhere, to a whole mass of people running in races and marching to the band. Have you been round the world?"

"Slightly. In an underground way."

"I suppose you saw my father in London. He is saving us from death."

"I don't remember your father. I find it very difficult to notice people, I am so concerned with the situation in our world today and the increasing and terrible death toll of beans."

"I could kill you. It would be easy for me to put my hand on you and squash you, or strike you with one of my books."

Erlene began to weep.

"How old am I? I've been waiting and waiting for you to tell me but you just sit there on the windowsill and never tell me. Why don't you tell me? And why has it all happened, that I am not allowed to speak anymore? Please, Uncle Blackbeetle, tell me! Where are you going? Don't go away! My mother is in the next room writing in her notebook. She is dotty and sad and she says good-night to each of the rooms in the house as if they were people. Please Uncle Blackbeetle, I would like to discover something, only to look out of the window into the sun-light and pounce upon the reason and capture it forever. There must be so many reasons flying in swarms around the sky and creeping secretly with their belly to the earth; I wish I had a net to trap them.

"Do you know the Scholar Gipsy, Uncle Black-beetle?"

There was silence then, everywhere. The birds stopped

singing, the blackbirds with the morning rain in their feathers and the magpies at their out-of-hours cocktail party in the gum trees, and the bellbird living in the big Canadian fir tree halfway down the hill, and from there taking control of the golden bell suspended from the sky, ringing it, as he is privileged to do, whenever he chooses, dingdong and it swings backward and forward in the air, invisibly, striking the bodies of dizzily flying insects who drop suddenly still, and lie with their feelers broken and their eyes closed, in the long yellow twists of grass.

The birds stopped singing, the wind stopped blowing, even the slightest wind that rustles the grass in the burned places near the railway line on the opposite hill.

"Hush!" Uncle Blackbeetle said. "Do you hear it?"

"I can't hear anything."

"Hush!"

"I'm hushing, but I can't hear anything. I'm not moving and I'm trying not to breathe, and my hands are here, on the windowsill. What is it?"

"It's the soldiers passing in twos and threes, with iron bands round their foreheads and little sachets of diseases and lavender flowers tied to their waists, and their teeth cleaned with white ash."

"Wood ash?"

"People ash."

"And swords of ribbonwood?"

83

"No swords."

"And medals, uniforms with medals, bright-red uniforms?"

"No medals, no bright-red uniforms, only the soldiers thin as the wind, in twos and threes in the dark."

"Is it death then?"

"Yes," said Uncle Blackbeetle.

And picking up his black apron he tied it by the two tapes around his waist, gathered his cutting, planing, polishing tools and set to work, choosing a shaded place on the windowsill. He was silent all afternoon while Erlene watched him, and sometimes, particularly when the birds seemed once more to stop their singing and the wind to fall still, she gazed beyond the window at the trees and the sky and she grew afraid, knowing that the soldiers were there in twos and threes, invisible, in their own dark, marching back and forth with no swords or medals or uniforms of bright-red cloth. And their teeth were cleaned with people ash. People ash? "Is it death, then?" she said again to Uncle Blackbeetle. He did not answer. He was tenderly lifting the shriveled bean body and placing it in its newly finished casket. He looked old and sad. As he bent down she saw that his apron was frayed at the edges. I will sew it for him, she thought. I will get scarlet cotton and a needle and sew a new hem, and up there near the pocket I will embroider a monogram so that he will belong somewhere and sing and run in races with a great mass of people close to him, and not ever be lonely.

Her mother came with a tray of food, scrambled egg, toast, tea, and two slices of ginger cake. Her mother was wearing a skirt and twin set; she looked like a schoolteacher. The veins on her hands were thick and raised, as if she had been chopping down trees, but she hadn't been chopping down trees, she had been sitting in the room across the passage writing in her notebook, Erlene knew, for sometimes she had heard a rustling like mice and straw and feathers and secrets, and it had been her mother turning the pages of her notebook, or writing letters to people who had vanished or died; or just sitting touching and folding sheets of paper.

"Erlene."

Her mother looked afraid as she spoke.

"Erlene, we can't live like this all the time, can we? Remember all the plans you were making for when you left school, and the party you were going to have, inviting Mifanwy—she's been asking after you, she wants to call and see you . . . you know the doctor who spoke to you last week up at the hospital . . . he wants you to go and talk to him . . . you will talk to him, won't you?"

Uncle Blackbeetle had gone home. He lived in the wall. His workshop was a lockup business so that when he left each night he had to be careful to lock the door and close the padlock and seal the windows. He always swept up the shavings from the windowsill, and tidied his tools, putting them in rows on his workbench, while in the room where the finished caskets lay he would sprinkle a perfume collected from the heads of the grasses growing around the front of the house, where the grass had not been cut since Grandad Bertram died. . . .

"Erlene, my dear, if you'll just move your lips to answer me, I'll understand. You'll talk to the doctor, won't you?"

She wished that Uncle Blackbeetle had not been telling her about the soldiers, yet she had been curious so often when silence came so suddenly with the birds hushing and the wind standing shadowless and still in the grass. She was longing for tomorrow when Uncle Blackbeetle would return and talk to her. She knew that even if she had to go up to the hospital and talk to the doctor, Uncle Blackbeetle would be there with her in case she felt afraid. He was her best friend. Mifanwy had been her best friend but she wasn't now, no one was her best friend, no people. . . .

"Just move your lips; it'll come; speech will come."

Her mother had a nibbling expression on her face, like a sheep. Erlene felt suddenly like crying at the thought of all the sheep out in the paddocks at night, the way they roam together on and on, this way and that, undecided, bleating, trying to find a sheltered spot; and then their calm, sitting side by side under the cold glass of the sky, in the night, when dew comes on the grass and the pink-gilled mushrooms are born, easily as breathing, spread white like circus tents on the slopes of the hill.

"Erlene, say something to me. People must speak, Erlene. Remember we used to read poetry together. . . ."

Erlene frowned. Why was her mother cross-questioning her, trying to find out her plans? Why did they so much want her to speak? Was it really so important to be able to speak? Hadn't there once been a placard hanging in the dunny for a joke, on the wall, SILENCE IS GOLDEN?

You would suppose, Erlene told herself, that the end of the world has come because I do not speak. People stare at me, waiting and waiting, because there are no words to calm them, no friendly words flying warm from my mouth. People dread silence because it is transparent; like clear water, which reveals every obstacle—the used, the dead, the drowned, silence reveals the cast-off words and thoughts dropped in to obscure its clear stream. And when people stare too close to silence they sometimes face their own reflections, their magnified shadows in the depths, and that frightens them. I know; I know.

"Do try. Just a little movement of your lips. Remember the speech training you used to have at school? 'We are standing on the grass watching the large cars pass; the large cars cannot harm us while we are standing on the grass.' 'Three gray geese in a green field grazing, gray were the geese and green was the grazing.' "

I could kill you as well as Uncle Blackbeetle, Erlene thought, staring at her mother, at her mouth where her lips still moved in that silly nibbling way as if she had changed to a sheep. Who was she?

"All the speech training, Erlene, remember, 'myriads of rivulets hurrying through the lawn. . . .' " That is not my mother, Erlene thought. This is not my home. This is the Dunedin Stock Exchange. Oh I wish it were all over, and that I had left school and was a student in the city, wearing brown brogues and a dirty brown raincoat and walking along the main street with books under my arm, folios, heavy books with small print, large note-books, lecture books with a crest on them which people use so that they may not be lonely.

Late that night when she was lying in bed, not sleep-ing, listening to the owls in the trees outside and the rustling of the opossums and the sniff-sniff of the hedge-hogs in the grass, sniffing and blowing like a man in the bathroom, her grandfather, perhaps her father who was rescuing the world; lying flat with her arms folded across her breast, as if she were dead; thinking now about what her mother had said to her—was it her mother?—about speaking and the doctor and standing on the grass watch-ing the large cars pass and the geese grazing in the fields and the rivulets with their workbags in their hands hurrying across the lawn, a shortcut to catch the morning train.

She began to feel afraid. What did it all mean?

When the sun had been shining and the light, as was its habit, had dipped its knife in the optimistic spread of day and traced it through the world, buttering and layering leaves and streets and people, the prospect of tomorrow and a doctor shaking her by the shoulders, commanding Speak Speak while Uncle Blackbeetle stood by unable to help, had not seemed so terrible, for she had faith in Uncle Blackbeetle, that he would take his little bag and his tools and come to some arrangement, sign treaties, with all the people who were trying to make her speak. But now in the dark with her hands crossed over her breast in an attitude of the dead, she remembered that Uncle Blackbeetle was old. He had not even the strength to inspect her dictionary. His days of traveling even as far as the hospital on the hill were finished now, and it was his task just to live in the hole by the wall and emerge during the day to his workshop on the windowsill, to care for the slain beans, even the tiniest ones who had died without opening their eyes and who were so small they would fit three at a time in one of the caskets; though Uncle Blackbeetle had told her that he did not approve of putting three at a time, and he never did so, for it was mass burial, he said.

"Mass loneliness, mass fear, mass burial," he said to her one day as he was working; but she did not fully understand him.

"What about the monograms and the flags?" she had asked.

But he did not answer except to repeat, "Mass loneliness, mass fear, mass burial."

As she lay in the dark her feeling of apprehension increased. Oh no, she could never go up to the hospital and have to talk to the doctor without Uncle Blackbeetle. Uncle Blackbeetle was the only one to talk to, here on the windowsill.

"Erlene, Erlene!"

It was her mother calling from the door, which she had opened softly; now she was tiptoeing over to the bed. In the light from the passage Erlene saw that her mother was wearing the Wincyette Woolworth's nightie which was too long and the tiny rosebuds spattered upon it gave her mother a childish appearance. Her face was pale. She had rubbed cream on her face and her skin shone, like the skin of a creature just emerged from the sea, or perhaps she had taken the literal meaning of the words on the jar of cream, *Vanishing*, and had applied it as a prelude to invisibility.

Perhaps she is my mother, Erlene thought.

In approaching the bed her mother tripped suddenly

over the trailing end of her nightie, and lurched forward clumsily.

"Erlene."

Suddenly the tears were running down her mother's cheeks as she leaned and clasped Erlene in her arms. Erlene's skin went cold and her heart beat fast at the sight of her mother's tears. Obstinately she kept her arms over her breast, as if she were dead, and refused to embrace her mother.

"Erlene. I think you will get better and speak to us. Just once a week you will be going up to the hospital to sit in a little room with Dr. Clapper, not to talk if you don't want to, just to sit and make friends with him. Would you like that, Erlene?"

Her mother smoothed the blankets, tucked them in, and tiptoed from the room, closing the door softly as if Erlene were asleep.

And it was not long before Erlene fell asleep and dreamed that the soldiers in twos and threes with bags of diseases and lavender tied at their waists, with iron bands round their foreheads, and their teeth cleaned with people ash, were passing to and fro in the night when all was silent, and then Uncle Blackbeetle looking sad and old in his frayed apron was turning from his work and glancing at her and saying, "Yes, yes," in answer to her question, "Is it Death?"

It was a clean morning with the sun making a sharp clop-clop noise like scrubbed clogs on stone, and in the hedge outside the blackbird, with so much light upon him that he nearly went up in smoke, was trilling joyously, dropping and catching notes like a spendthrift millionaire. The sun had been up a long time, rising out of the sea, with its face toward Weston and Waiareka, where it had slept the night, just behind the saleyards and the old rusty branch-railway line, and the one or two farms near the foothills. Bees were out in the grass and clover, sheep had found their day's grazing and were hard at work, their noses to the short tough grass on the already burned slopes spilled here and there with gray dusty earth from the scampered beginnings of rabbit burrows that for some reason had never been finished; horses stood gleaming and steaming in what shade they could find, flicking the dark-blue zooming flies that strayed upon their necks or flanks from their feasting place in the whirled cones of straw-filled dung; other flies hummed their steady rounds, poised so far from the glistening leaves of the silver poplar, oak, willow; blobs of resin melted, trickled down the trunks of the pine trees where the dry cones cracked like whips; tiny spiders were swinging and crawling and climbing silk threads hand over hand to the sky.

Trains were whistling, cars carrying milk cans were rattling along the road; a flock of sheep, on the road since dawn, was approaching unseen, but the bleating and barking and the cries of the drover sounded from near the bend in the road, and clouds of dust were rising from the hidden commotion.

Down in the harbor the dredge was at work, clanking and clattering; saws were whining and screaming in the sawmill; chutes racketing a-tick a-tick in the flour mill; auctioneers were hammering and shouting.

Pencils and rubbers were whispering, typewriters were tapping, machines were jiving, people were talking.

People were talking.

All under the stealthy sky; and water everywhere was shining.

Erlene was awake, lying still. The shadow of the outside world moved across the drawn blind and the sunlight revealed the crisscross skeleton on tinsel upon which the navy-blue blind was woven. The outside world was striding by in giant boots, treading on insects—snails carved and luminous, ants shouldering the bodies of their dead and struggling through the tall burned leafless forest, blackbeetles—Erlene jumped from her bed, ran to the window, pulled up the blind, which sprang with a snapping noise nearly to the roof, and put the entire room at the mercy of the light; and opening the window and peering out onto the sill, Erlene looked for Uncle

Blackbeetle. He was not there. Then she remembered that this day was his holiday. Immediately she felt depressed and lonely. She pulled down the blind and was about to get back into bed when her mother came to the door.

"Not up yet, Erlene?"

Not up! (And water everywhere was shining.)

"Remember we're going to see the doctor today. He's going to make friends with you."

(All under the stealthy sky.)

Why was her mother not real? Why was she always writing in the front room, and touching the furniture, lightly, as if her fingers were a wand, and why did she look so strange every morning with her eyes dark and her face very pale as if she had spent a long time in a world without light, as if her kind of sleep were a kind of pit beneath the earth? And why did she insist every day upon turning, shaking, folding, smoothing the clouds in the sky as if they were sheets upon a slept-in rumpled bed? Why did she want to stay forever in this house, and never move to another town and never look for another husband?

Also, why did everyone consider it so necessary for people to talk?

The sun sizzled in her head, like a trout cooking, and the burned skin peeling off, and she began to cry.

"Erlene dear, there's nothing to be afraid of, you will

just meet a nice kind doctor and sit with him in a nice room, with the sun shining in the window."

The sun.

They walked up the back way to the hospital, past the nurses' home and the laundry and into the cool brown corridor. Erlene's mother went in first to talk to the doctor, then she came out and sat beside Erlene. She had streaky patches like red sand on the skin of her neck and her face was red.

The doctor came out to the waiting room. He was tall, with fair hair like batter mixture only dry, and he wore a long white coat with three holes in the right sleeve and a dead tiger moth in one of the pockets, deep in the corner beside the fluff and biscuit crumbs.

He came up to Erlene, smiling cheerfully, stretching out his hand to shake hers.

"Hello there."

Why did he say *Hello there?* Why not just *Hello?* Anyone would think she was over the boundary in another part of the world for the doctor to hail her like that. He might just as well have yodeled or cupped his hands about his mouth and coo-eed.

"I'm Dr. Clapper."

He grasped her hand and shook it heartily.

"And you're Erlene?"

He answered himself.

"That's right, you're Erlene."

It was a presumption, but she did not protest; how could he be so sure when she was not sure herself?

"If you come in here, Erlene, in this nice sunny room, I'll have a little talk to you."

Why did her mother and the doctor need to emphasise the "niceness" and the "sunniness" of the room?

Erlene followed Dr. Clapper into the nice sunny room and sat down facing him.

"You're going to come and see me often, aren't you?" he asked, again replying to himself, "Of course you are. I'm not going to bother you with all those examinations you had when you visited the hospital once before, you've had all those and you won't want them again, will you? No, of course not. I'm just going to have little chats with you."

He leaned forward with his eyes suddenly glistening in a hungry way,

"Is there anything you want to tell me?"

Erlene stared at him seriously, thinking, I wonder what Uncle Blackbeetle will say when I tell him. I will tell him as soon as I go home.

And once more the doctor talked to himself, smiling gently, and absentmindedly fingering the three little holes in the sleeve of his white coat, as if to say, See, I am human, I have three little holes in the sleeve of my white coat, so it follows . . . doesn't it . . . it follows . . . good god what happens when you reach the brink and there is nothing following?

"Well perhaps there is nothing you want to tell me today. Will you write a story for me? Your mother tells me you like reading."

Dr. Clapper leaned forward again, with an air of excitement, as if he had discovered a gold mine, "My word, there must be lots of stories going round and round in your head—eh?"

Erlene wished he would say it was time for her to go, but he kept her there, even though she did not speak, and she felt annoyed that he had not actually asked her to speak, why hadn't he when everybody else seemed to want her to speak? What was so special about him?

She frowned. He was staring hard at her but when she caught him staring he looked away and pretended to be gazing at the wall. Then he snipped a blue pen from his pocket, unscrewed the cap, tested the ink on his hand, glancing over at Erlene as if to say, See, I am human, I am testing the ink on my hand; then he began to write on a sheet of paper, with his hand moving quickly in his smart doctor's writing. He covered a whole page with writing, and then he looked up, and smiled.

"See, I'm writing my story. Now I bet you have a little story to write, haven't you?"

He did not seem to understand that Erlene did not want to write little stories, that she had never wanted to write little stories, and her head was not one of the Southern Lakes with stories whizzing round and round in it like speedboats. Besides, for all his talk of writing his story, Dr. Clapper made sure that she did not read it Erlene knew why. He had only been writing his estimate of her.

"Or perhaps you have a picture to paint? You are too old to make houses for me out of blocks, aren't you?"

He tried to sound convinced that she was too old, bu it was evident that he believed she was child enough to make houses out of blocks, even to play in a sand pit o: make mud pies.

He was writing swiftly now, covering another shee of hospital paper. When he had finished he put the sheet into a buff-colored folder, closed it, wrote a number carefully, on the outside, then putting his elbows on th table he smiled at Erlene.

"We're going to be friends, aren't we old thing?"

Old thing!

Erlene was shocked. He scarcely knew her, and he wa trying to be familiar, saying they were old friend perhaps he was like the wild men she had heard of, wh put their hands up girls' clothing.

She was afraid. Uncle Blackbeetle, save me, sh thought. Uncle Blackbeetle save me; for Dr. Clapper wa resting his hand on her shoulder, and seeing her to th door, and saying Good-bye old thing, old thing; ar even when he had taken his hand away from her shoulder she could feel the ghost of the pressure of it, and all the way home she kept seeing his eyes, shining blue and green like the inside of a paua shell lying on the beach in the sun. She felt ashamed and afraid and sad, because when she looked out of the window to talk to Uncle Blackbeetle he was still not there, and she had forgotten that today was his holiday. And the soldiers kept passing in twos and threes wearing the iron bands around their foreheads and the sachets of lavender and diseases at their waists, and their teeth shone white from the cleaning with people ash. And Erlene started to cry because there was no one to be friends with her and protect her.

There were also two speckled hawks with burning glass eyes who spent all day sitting on the top of the mountain choosing their victims and preparing for the night, when they swooped and struck, not at birds or baby rabbits, as all the world seemed to believe, but at people in their sleep, for Erlene knew that when people were asleep their minds were covered by a golden cloth, richly embroidered, which served the useful purpose of protecting those who slept from the pollen of death which was shaken down each night from the sky, from the death flowers growing everlastingly in the fields of night. Sometimes the two speckled hawks, flying together, swooped down and carried away the embroidered cloth to the mountain places, and in the morning the people who had been robbed of their safeguard could not be wakened, or they were dead or mad; other times the coverlet was torn, and the death dust penetrated the dreaming mind, paralyzing or killing tiny parts of it, in fact *speckling* the mind with death. Erlene knew that a time came when the people who suffered in this way changed to speckled hawks, sitting on the mountaintop, choosing. . . .

It frightened her. There was no end to it. Every night the hawks were flying down, entering people, leaving people, bearing away the precious coverlets, and soon there would not be enough room on all the mountaintops in the world for the speckled deaths with their burning glass eyes and the screams in their throats.

I don't scream, Erlene thought. I *won't* scream. I will lie here under the blankets with my head under the pillow, and not look up if I hear a scratching on my window or the flutter of wings against the pane. Uncle Blackbeetle will save me, secret in his little house in the wall. Tomorrow I will talk to him.

She curled under the bedclothes with her head under the pillow. I wonder what the Scholar Gipsy is doing now, she thought, and then she said to herself, But he would not manage in this country, he would get lost in the bush and not know how to boil the billy, and if he spent his time lolling about in rivers "trailing in the cool stream his fingers wet" he would quickly be swept away by the current, his boat would capsize and he would be drowned.

So she thought for a while about the Scholar Gipsy, and for a time she forgot about the hawks.

Then she remembered that she could not speak.

I cannot speak, she said. They will not let me speak. What will happen to me if I cannot speak anymore, all my life? Then she thought of Dr. Clapper, and she grew afraid. Had his eyes made her pregnant? Was it true that men could look at you in a special way and make you pregnant?

She felt her tummy; there seemed to be a swelling there. She had not had her monthlies for a long time. What did it mean? Was Jesus inside her? Would he be born one day, one morning, in the little shed halfway down the garden where the apples were stored, and the sacks of wheat for the fowls and the garden rake and spade; where the errand boy from the Star Stores left the weekly order—goods smelling of sandsoap, carbolic, vanilla? The shed needed painting, especially the door, which hung on one hinge and would not shut, and in late autumn the floor was thick with drifts of dead leaves, and the roof leaked, and the acorns and the rain pelted down.

And perhaps then she would be lying in the shed, on the dead leaves, cradling the baby in her arms and wearing a blue nightie, and all the neighbors would be hurrying up the drive and through the rusty bedstead gate to the shed, bringing their gifts. And the mayor would visit, wearing the municipal chain, and the Governor General would take time off from his garden parties on the lawn of Government House to visit her with his wife; and the headmistress, and the chairman of the Board of Governors, and the teachers from the school—Miss Walters and Miss Merchant, and the girls, the prefects and the gawky little third-formers waiting to be balloted into their schoolhouses—all would come to see her and the baby. . . .

There was a sudden rustling outside, a tapping at the window. Erlene held her breath in suspense. Who was it? The hawks? The soldiers? Dr. Clapper? If she was going to be frightened in this way, she thought, the child would die inside her and she would walk around in the world with a smell of death surrounding her, and people would be afraid to come near her, in case they would be infected. And deep inside her the baby would be so still, and never learn how to breathe or walk or open its fists and put out its hand to touch and grasp, and it would never be able to see or talk or cry out when it sensed the two speckled hawks advancing upon it from the mountaintop or when the soldiers of death passed in twos and threes. The dead thing inside her would not be a baby; it would be a walnut, a piece of driftwood, the dead limb of a tree, a small bitter green apple snapped off and lying in the wet grass, with the fringe and crown of the dead blossom still attached to it and never leaving it. . . .

Erlene slept.

Her mother, coming into the room and seeing the girl hidden under the bedclothes, loosened the blankets over her, and going to the window she opened it at the bottom to let in the night air, all the time interfering, interfering, as mothers do. She did not know of the hawks and the soldiers in twos and threes and the extra danger because of the baby; and it distressed her that the next morning Erlene seemed more ill than usual, sitting dully by the window, not looking up when her mother entered, not touching her food when it was brought to her, though her mother said, enticingly, as she thought, "See, it's on the pretty tray cloth which you yourself worked at school."

Erlene began to cry. How could her mother know of the terrible fear that in the night, after her mother had loosened the bedclothes and exposed her body to the night air, the hawks had entered the room and torn the embroidered cloth and speckled Erlene's mind with Death?

9
—

He went to the park.

The gate was pulled to.

He was found to be insane.

Was he?

I think that there is a mistake.

That is the reason I am here.

Shape pleases; sob bitterly; rattrap; made dull; vague guess; tough feeling; five voices; this season; those zebras; eighth theme; wreathe them; fish shop; pull lightly; calm moments; soapbox; mob pressure; must do; did take; duke goes; vague kind; enough vases; love fully; this zoo; those seats; both those; breathe through; oasis; opera arrangements; the hour; the apple; two ears; I saw an opening; how awful . . .

Yes, Edward thought, reading from his borrowed book on Practical Speech Training. The words are hard enough to pronounce even when one has the power of speech. It is a treacherous path from incoherence to lucidity, from the meaningless useless obstacles of love fully, this zoo, five voices, wreathe them, shape pleases, to the clear wonder of His glory not extenuated wherein he was worthy, nor his offenses enforced, for which he suffered death. "Though in the wayes of fortune or understanding or conscience thou have been benighted till now, wintred and frozen, clouded and eclypsed, smothered and stupefied till now . . . And I can gather out of thy word so good testimony of the hearts of men, as to find *single hearts docile* and *apprehensive* hearts; hearts that *can*, hearts that have learnt; wise hearts, in one place, and in another, in a great degree wise perfit hearts. . . ."

Edward put down the book of Speech Training and again considered Vera's letter. The news that Erlene was unable to speak seemed a threat, as the disabilities of others often do, to Edward himself and his project, his arrangement of the human race in a follow-my-leader of chains which would ultimately be shaken free, weightless, transparent, each link burdened only with dazzle and wholeness as if it were a drop of dew on a leaf of nasturtium or foxglove or dahlia. . . .

"Get the flowers in my grave," he said.

"She must regain her speech. They must do all they can for her, quickly. The loss of the speech of one person —the fact that she is my daughter is irrelevant—means the beginning of defeat for us all. It is many years since I heard Erlene speak. It does not matter whether she was in the habit of uttering the incoherences of this season, 'Calm moment, He was found to be insane, Was he, love fully, this zoo,' or whether she has used words as patterns of communication and survival like,

> "Oh reason not the need! Our basest beggars
> are in the poorest things superfluous. . . .
> man's life is cheap as beasts.

" 'Thou owest the worm no silk, the beast no hide, the sheep no wool, the cat no perfume. . . . thou art the thing itself; unaccommodated man is no more but such a poor bare, forked animal as thou art. . . .' "

What she has been saying in the years I have been absent is irrelevant as long as she has been speaking; now her loss of speech reminds me how death, silence, the enemy, is trying to outwit me in my task of leaving warning notices inside those who share my blood. Nothing must be allowed to silence our voices. We must be allowed to make our cries of pain and joy, our singing, murmuring, moaning, our everyday requests, statements, questions, greetings, good-byes; our deceits, flatteries, curses. We must call out to one another from mountaintop to mountaintop in language which grows more complicated than the first coo-ee or yodel; across seas and deserts flashing words instead of mirrors and lights; and in our final desperation we must speak or scream our message to those who sit and lie near us, touching skin to skin. . . .

106

And Erlene? With that secret confidence which people have in their ability to work miracles in situations when all other remedies have failed—we believe that the madman with the loaded gun, threatening to destroy those who try to capture him, will surrender his weapon to us alone if we approach him; we believe that a criminal will confess his guilt to us, if only the authorities will let us talk to him; that we can persuade the silent to speak to us, only to us; it is a secret charm which we all imagine that we possess . . . So Edward believed that if he were to visit Erlene and talk to her, then she would naturally answer him, as if she had never been deprived of her speech. She would talk to him; how could she do otherwise?

If I were there, he said to himself, in the same room, sitting beside her, smiling at her, there would simply be no question of loss of speech; why, she would surely talk to me—*to me!*

Having thus italicized himself, he grew curious, and stared in his dressing-table mirror. He frowned. In spite of his desire to rescue the human race he always became depressed at the reminder that he himself was human; and now, alone with his mirror, with his hands resting upon the egg-shaped top of the dressing table and his face close to the glass, he could not ignore the evidence of mortality presented by the undignified, trivial jar of pomade, which he rubbed into his scalp

107

daily; the ointment which he used to treat the pain in his right shoulder; the tiny box of corn plasters; the hair-brush, no longer used, lying on its back with its oil-stained feelers in the air like some extinct overfed insect. And then his face in the mirror, seen in waves of sickly yellow light from the fog outside which grasped its share of him even though the window was shut top and bottom; the fog lay in his mouth like a smelling staining beast occupying its cavern.

Edward could not understand why he who had so much power, whose presence would inspire his dumb child to speech, should be forced to endure the petty mutilations of time and light, should have no defense against the perpetual assault, the stones thrown, the axes striking, day after day, and the secret traps and covered pits laid maliciously in his path, and the trip wires to death which gradually surrounded him and which one day would make him afraid to move, or so careful that he stepped one inch at a time, making his perilous day's journey from his bed to his bathroom to his filed histories to his dressing table to his bathroom to his bed.

He was tired. In spite of the changed prescription for his glasses, his eyes kept watering, the stuff trickling down his cheeks like unbidden tears. He would draw his large white handkerchief from his pocket and rub his cheeks, crooking his forefinger and pressing his fist against his cheek as if to conceal or catch the tears, and when he was sitting in the library with the old news-papers about him steaming with compost of decayed news, and people happened to see him wiping his eyes, they would whisper facetiously, "Weeping, Edward. The past gets you like that."

But Edward would be conscious only of a feeling of misery as if something had got out of his control, and he did not know what it was.

His eyes watered now as he gazed in the mirror. He was suddenly filled with a feeling of love—for himself, for Erlene, or for the human race, he did not know which, but like a lighthouse keeper whose beacon shines upon three wrecks and he must choose which to rescue first, not realizing that he has been deceived and there is only one wreck, Edward chose Erlene as the object of his rescue, his love. He thought, In spite of the fact that we have been separated for so many years, she will know me when she sees me, she will talk to me. It is not true what they say—that people absent from each other for so long put on a strangeness; I do not believe the stories. I know that after years of wandering and warring and loving, the Greek sailors were recognized by their families immediately they came ashore. For Penelope there was never any swineherd who suddenly cast off a disguise and cried, I am Ulysses; there was only Ulysses; only and always.

Ulysses?

Edward traced his hand over his bald head and winced as he touched a raw spot, a tiny pimple. He squeezed it. It spurted a niggardly white offering between his thumb and forefinger. He sighed. Wiping his eyes again, he folded his wife's letter, looking curiously at the outside with its ferocities of ominous postmarkings, Address All Letters Clearly, Watch Grass Fires, Take Your Litter Home, Burn All Evidence, Lock All Doors, Bury All Bodies . . . and then, eagerly, trying to forget his unaccustomed family involvement, he opened his other letter written in an unknown handwriting and postmarked (again with perforated warnings) Dunedin, New Zealand.

The letter read,

Quarter Street,
Dunedin. January.

Dear Mr. Glace,

I was interested to get your letter telling me about our family history. We have always been interested in our ancestors and while my husband was alive we kept in touch with his relations in the North of England, but we have lost touch now and the last I heard was a Christmas card some years back. You say that you might be coming to New Zealand to go on with your research. If you come to Dunedin we would be very pleased to put you up. There is just myself, my two grown-up daughters and two sons and the house is roomy. With reference to what you say in your letter, it is interesting to know that we have clever people in the family—I believe my husband's uncle was gifted. No, we do not mind if you mention those members of the family who have not quite lived up to expectations, for of course every family has its black sheep, but as far as the affair of Aunt Margaret is concerned, I hope you realize that she was an aunt by marriage only, and not really a relation.

What made you choose our family for your research? We are just ordinary people but I know we have many distinguished relatives and while my husband was alive he often talked of tracing them. I read in the newspapers about the Wallace Strang you mentioned. He is not any connection with us at all.

> Hoping to hear more news from
> you in due course,
> I remain,
> Yours faithfully,
> CLARA STRANG

Edward smiled as he read and folded the letter and replaced it in the envelope. Already he felt for Clara Strang that overwhelming love which he gave so freely to members of the Strang family as if it belonged to them by right. He had never bestowed such feeling upon his wife or child or anyone he knew. It seemed to him to be a kind of love which arrived to him from an unknown source, and which he held in trust on the mysterious condition that he should not use it, only contemplate it and care for it before he passed it on to the chosen people, the Strangs, most of whom were never even aware that they had received it. Edward knew that his chosen family might look upon his interest in them as the eccentricity of a wealthy man (his income was perpetual) with little better to concern him than the study (spy spy) of other people's history. On the other hand, they would perhaps be pleased and flattered that he had chosen them. Clara Strang had seemed grateful, as if she had received an unexpected present. He smiled. She did not know that the unexpected present was his love. Then he frowned, as his eyes watered again, and he drew his handkerchief to wipe them.

"It's the strain of everything," he said to himself. "Life is becoming too complicated, too much is being demanded of me. . . ."

First there was this letter from his wife asking him to return home in the hope that his presence might prompt Erlene into speech. (His wife had made no such request, yet he was so convinced that he could persuade Erlene to talk that he now believed, after thinking about the matter, that his wife had asked him to return, had stressed that everything depended upon him.)

Next there was this letter from Clara Strang inviting

112

him to stay when he visited New Zealand. And there would be other letters too, from the living Strangs, all expressing concern or delight that he had chosen to investigate their history, all claiming baronetcies and disclaiming criminals while agreeing that black sheep were part of every family; soon the letters would be in every day's mail. He would not be able to escape from them. Was it wise of him to have moved thus from the dead to the living? Was his concern for the human race really so deep that he could now face the living, and after that, the unborn, without disaster to himself? Was it worthwhile pursuing the struggle when even if one person in the world became deaf, blind, dumb, or afflicted with the silence of the insane, all the forces which threatened to destroy the human race moved in to try to break once and for all the entire pattern of communication; when day after day all the brave people of the world who listened, looked, danced, spoke, sang, were in danger of becoming cripples of loneliness and silence with their language decayed, the words overgrown and no longer cared for, not pruned or picked or marketed, arranged in shining bowls in shaded rooms of the mind? And why, Edward wondered, had his daughter Erlene been chosen to represent the terrible silence which threatened mankind? Who had chosen her?

He felt confused. The false tears rolled down his

113

cheeks, diluting and making mockery of his genuine grief.

"I am truly at war now," he told himself. The hobby of a gentleman (yes, a gentleman) became first his passion, then his excuse for escape, then his excuse for survival, for grafting himself like the extra inadequate bit of human skin that he was, upon some part of humanity where he would not need to prove his gallantry, his manliness, his unselfishness; and now it has become his battlefield with death encroaching on all sides piercing defenses, destroying communications . . . while the soldier weeps plastic tears and awards medals for the purest vomit. . . .

The letter from the Lake District the next morning alarmed him.

Dear Mr. Glace,

Thank you for your kind letter and the trouble you have taken to enquire into our ancestry. Yes, Lyndon is living at Peckham, I mean he was living at Peckham, for he died today, and this letter is to ask if you would care to attend his funeral on our behalf, on Tuesday 10 a.m. I have talked the matter over with my wife, and she has agreed that since Lyndon is one of the last of the family, someone interested ought to attend his funeral. Unfortunately we cannot leave our farm but considering your kind letter and your interest in our concerns we have decided to ask you to do us this favour. From the tone of your letter we gathered that you are an upright man.

I enclose a letter of introduction to Lyndon's wife, Georgina, as she may not receive it as promptly as you receive this. My wife has explained your kind errand which I hope you will have the time to perform, thus to earn the heart-felt gratitude of the Strang family.

We would gladly give you any information which you require, but my wife has asked me to point out that the Wallace Strang who was tried recently in the Old Bailey is not a relation of ours.

Yours sincerely,
EDGAR ELVIN STRANG

Inside the envelope was a sealed letter addressed, "To Georgina Strang, 3 Prudence Avenue Peckham, London. S.E. 21."

Edward read the letter:

DEAR GEORGIE,

It was a shock to us to get your telegram today. Lyndon seemed so young and not a man who would be taken so soon. Edgar and I send our deepest sympathy to you and Molly. It must be terrible for Molly to lose her father when she is still a schoolgirl. But these seem

115

mere idle words, don't they, when you start to write about bereavement because nothing can recall the dead; they are with God according to His Plan. Edgar and I want you to know that we are thinking of you in your sorrow.

You will understand that we cannot get down to the funeral, and we are asking Mr. Edward Glace who will give you this letter, to kindly represent us, as in a way he is almost a member of the family. He has studied our ancestry right back to earliest times, and is still studying it and wrote to us recently about his interest in us. At first Edgar and I thought it was rather cheek for him to be trying to find out all about us, and then Edgar said we should be flattered because he wouldn't be studying the family unless it was noble and ancient and talented for what use would there be in studying an ordinary family? Excuse all this detail at a time like this but it is best for us to explain about Mr. Glace. After all, you never know do you? We feel proud to ask him to represent us at Lyndon's funeral, although we wish of course that we could get away from the farm to be with you and Molly and I'm only sorry we have not been able to get down to London more often. It must be years since we saw you or Lyndon or Molly and cards at Christmas tell absolutely nothing do they? It is terrible isn't it, how it all happens, from one moment to the next, but only on the

116

last day shall the canvas be unrolled and God show the Reason Why.

> Not till the loom is silent,
> and the wheels have ceased to fly,
> shall God unroll the canvas,
> and explain the reason why.

All our love to you and Molly and our sympathy in your sorrow.

Your loving sister-in-law,
JANET

After Edward had read the letter he found an envelope, retyped the address, and resealed the letter. He knew that the person who might be known as the "real" Janet Strang did not write the letter signed by her, nor did her husband write the one where his signature flourished its E loops like lassos trying to round up the stampeding platitudes. In their use of words they appeared only as dull parched souls caked with the footprints of an extinct education in grammar and written expression; prints made so long ago that any of the real lark-feelings, the outpourings of genuine family affection, were satisfied to build their nests in the ready-made hollows, and never to abandon them for the sky and the true place of their singing.

That is why it is important, Edward told himself as

117

he put aside the letters, that Erlene should regain her power of speech; and why Edgar Elvin, Clara, Georgina, Janet Strang must be cared for and loved in secret, in my special way, for they have never found their power of speech. Perhaps sometime in the future the written and spoken words of this ordinary family will touch like lances upon the skin of those nearest to them, will draw blood from the selected wound, will penetrate and unfold the flower closed upon its own heart; but sun and lances are so old, and dead, and this is tomorrow, it is the time of the flash in the sky, the deep burn of words which destroy all power to create, the time of a first-degree language so articulate that the vision of it results in physical blindness, and those who have spoken one word of it are struck dumb and forbidden ever to speak again. How do I know that my daughter has not advanced to a place in Time (an architectural conception to suit our choice of dormitory, cubicle, bedroom, kitchen, temple, tent, coffin) populated, governed, furnished, threatened by spoken words which test and flash in the sky and strike dumb those with no defense against them? Who knows that Erlene has not strayed into the future (as I, her father, have spent my time straying in the past), where few human beings have survived (do you not see my Strang family sitting silent in the adjectival temple?) the tyrannical practices of the ruling words, and where those who are still alive are now forever silent, subjected to the very words which in the past flew so merrily, mightily, heedlessly, from between their lips?

Occupied by his fantasy (for fantasies move in and take over territory, and, like words, set up their form of dictatorship) Edward sat quite still in his armchair with the letters forgotten on the table beside him. He thought, I wonder if I could measure the extent of my power, if I could build an unassailable defense against the future, if I could entomb myself, yes, entomb myself in order to prevent Death from reaching me, if I could sham the death of the entire human race in order to fool Death as he passes by in his search for victims? Should I make a marble image of my entranced family of Strangs? Have I been right in concentrating upon their history, their movement forward in time with their accumulation of energy of being which, I have hoped, is to be proof against final destruction, even if the future promises them nothing but silence in the adjectival temple, the street of slogan, the city of distorted meaning? Perhaps I should have been wiser if I had painted this family, if I had created in oils or watercolors one flat captured image like a shut paper lantern which the mind could unfold and fill with light and hang in the darkest areas of Time. Or I might have made music from my Strangs, beginning and ending them with my own power, providing them with completeness and form so that their music encompassed space with the notes driving downward and upward, set and pinnacled in stone, like stalactites and stalagmites occurring in the caves of Time. It has been a long laborious task searching out the details of this one family, and now that I have reached the living representatives, I do wonder if I should not have chosen a form of art—vivid, swift (like death) instead of becoming involved with the dullness and diffuseness of people's everyday lives. Edgar Elvin Strang. Clara Strang. Janet Strang. Georgina Strang. A visit to a funeral. A visit to New Zealand, forty sheep to every human being, surrounding each one in a charm of indecision, conformity, and coziness; and panic, the everyday drive to death along the roads by the tussock-covered hills, the cabbage trees, the bush; not the dark death that inhabits my own mind as a product of the northern hemisphere, but a sunny, dusty death, a kind of death amidst stupidity, futility, panic. I remember now that in the southern hemisphere one finds the true conception of death as something unnecessary, evil, brought about by laziness, dust, sunlight, and the tiny minds going mad because there is no way out of the paddock and the fence is too strong to break; it is a terrible death in the sun with the dry cabbage leaves crackling like fire and the grass burned from the hills, and the browned bodies lying still and sprawled upon the beaches where those lavish blue-green shells

—Vera said they were pauas—scoop up the sunlight. . . .

I understand why Vera stays in New Zealand, why the land is her true lover. Yet how she must suffer the ordinariness and diffuseness of everyday living. A daughter struck dumb. What a flash of vision and significance in her life! How Vera will profit from it! Well I certainly remember her, I remember her hairpins, the crinks in them, and the way she insisted that hairpins, pins, buttons, domes lost in beds between sheets under tables in cracks between floorboards down bathroom sinks, all undergo a natural process of dissolution; like bodies after death; tiny packets of hairpins between my finger and thumb. . . .

Edward sighed. People do sigh, in fiction, and in real life after they have been trapped in a fantasy and a sudden noise, movement, a physical demand, sets them free to rejoin the insistent clatter and irrelevance of day-to-day living. Edward sighed again. He realised that noises, shadows, even his own body, were in a continual state of jealousy toward him, as they are toward all human beings. Even the furniture of his room—the table, the bed, the chairs, the light bulb, everything which the landlord termed "fixtures and fittings" experienced this dark uneasiness at his every thought and act; while within his own body his arms were jealous of his hands, his head was jealous of his belly, his eyes could

121

not bear the fact that they were not ears; his mouth moaned that it was not his fingertips touching; there was no satisfaction anywhere; there was war.

No room or body is peaceful, not in any part of the world where human beings are, for people have such power, which spreads to the objects surrounding them and concerning them, and no one speaks the truth when he asserts that he keeps himself to himself; there is no sealed container.—How neat everything would be then! Edward said to himself. No past, present, future. No Strangs.

Well, it was the Strangs who concerned him now. The present Strangs and a funeral on a dark winter's day.

He decided to visit Georgina Strang at Prudence Avenue. It did not worry him that he had opened, read, resealed, and readdressed the letter meant for her. It was Edward's practice, whenever he was confronted with a sealed letter, to open it (by steam), read it, and reseal it, then post it. He was afflicted with an enormous appetite for human news especially when it was pro-vided in the intimacies of letters from stranger to stranger; news of births, deaths gathered in that way gave him a feeling of belonging and sharing which news gathered in the ordinary way, told from friend to friend, did not give him; the beckoning of a friend, whispered confidences, heart-to-heart talks at midnight,

122

letters written to him "because it's news and I must tell you, you must know," only increased his feeling of isolation.

I can't help being a squalid personality, he said to himself as he prepared for his visit. That's my excuse. I can't help it. I only wish the furniture did not take command of me, and that with all my money (from its secret source) I sometimes thought of buying a teapot in which the tea leaves did not keep escaping through the spout into my cup! And I wish that I could believe that the marmalade I buy, again cheaply, does not contain dyed plastic made to resemble the rind of lemon and orange and placed sparsely here and there in the mixture in order to complete the deception on the label, *Wundagold Marmalade*. But perhaps that is a good beginning to a day in which I shall celebrate a squalid event such as Death.

He took out his map of London. He lived in the north of the city and seldom consciously ventured south of the river, and had just a vague idea that it was a place of suburbs and power stations and men in cloth caps and rotten oranges; but he could not be sure. Certainly many times he had traveled to south London for his research work but on those occasions the world passed by unnoticed—he read while he traveled, for he belonged to the group of people who are not so disconcerted by motion and the primitive fear that they are being borne to a destination other than that printed upon their ticket, that they must glance apprehensively through the windows of trains and buses, trying to note and remember the details of the surrounding countryside, only to get a clue in order that when they arrive in foreign territory they shall not feel totally lost; no, Edward was one of the aristocratic, pompous few who do not seem to care, and what is more he did *read* in the train and bus and not merely have the hollow of his eyes domed by the protruding black shapes of words and fixed there in the deceiving attitude adopted by those who like to read when they travel, who are not disturbed by motion, yet whose eyes refuse to submit to the conventional left-to-right discipline of the mechanics of reading and whose stomachs feel unhappy in the midst of journeys. Oh the persistent pampering necessary for the human body! Nothing but jealousy, threatened rebellion, secret practices, spy rings, war, war; and day after day the whimpering sly demands which exercise more power and cause more destruction than armed combat.

But to be able to read in the bus was only a slight victory for Edward, since it made him unfamiliar with his surroundings.

He took out his map of London, plotted his course to Prudence Avenue, carefully noting the numbers of the buses, and judging the time he would be delayed at roundabouts and other areas of dense traffic, until he had calculated the exact time he would arrive at Prudence Avenue. Then dressing in a white shirt, dark suit and dark tie, and a heavy black overcoat, he went from his room down the stairs sniffing in his customary way at the characteristic brown desolate-archway musty-grief smell which inhabited the foot of the stairs, just inside the front door, beside the mirrored table where each morning the letters were placed, arranged like aces of spades; a smell that was the property, the fixture and fitting of all houses with rooms to let that Edward had ever known. Before he settled down finally (though his coffin waited, biding its time) in this flat he had twice stayed in a family household and he had been surprised, almost alarmed, to find that family households were not permeated with this peculiar smell. Did the practice of containing a complete family set the house free from this terrible soap-and-death atmosphere? Or was the atmosphere something which one by one the inhabitants brought with them when they came to stay and which remained when they left, as much a part of their discarded property as the worn shaving brush, the rusty razor blades dropped behind the bath, the empty coat hangers hanging light-headed in the closed serious wardrobe, the stray shirt that came back from the laundry too late to be claimed and found its way

amongst the landlady's sheets and towels and pillow-
cases and was given the name "X's" shirt, and X identi-
fied as "the man who stayed on the top floor in that
small room with the shilling meter outside, the man
before the man before the man there now. . . ."

"The man before the man before the man there now."

"See," Edward said triumphantly as the thought
flashed through his mind though not destroying him
utterly, "see how the continuity of the human race
demands expression, even by landladies!"

He opened the front door, turned his coat collar up
against the bitter wind, making a theatrical gesture as if
he were part of the opening scene in a film, one of those
shadowy black-and-white films where music thuds like
cardboard made to resemble wood but left in the rain
and dampened so that the notes can be removed in strips
and fall to pieces in layered waddings of sound. It was
a grim day. Winter was putting on the pressure all right.
It was the kind of day, Edward noted, when funerals
seemed to pass in the streets, nothing but funerals, coffins containing old bronchial fluey men and women. He
longed for spring or summer. He longed to be stepping
gaily into the street, nearly colliding with the hordes of
fat pregnant women who in spring and summer
prowled splendid as she-cats up and down in the sun.
He longed for the lilacs to be in bloom in that garden
near the corner, just by the fence; and then for the

126

season to be full summer with the tar melting on the pavement and the sweating strawberries carefully accommodated in their pale splintered boxes in the market stalls, and the barrows topped with blood-spattered blackheart cherries; and in the long evenings riotous with pop music and gunfire from television sets, in all the little back gardens the satisfied shirt-sleeved men making proud public water with their permitted hoses . . . that was summer.

Do I need a briefcase for the funeral? Edward wondered. After all, I have done serious research into the family. And does not a briefcase signify research? Into other people's pockets, hearts or histories?

He hurried back into the house and found his empty briefcase.

Now some people, he said to himself as once again he crossed the frontier of the smell just inside the front door, may wonder why I choose this part of London to live in. I could be in a more select area. I could be in a more comfortable flat—Hampstead, Bromley, the West End—a mews flat surrounded by the odor of horse manure and spilt cocktails. But does it matter where I live when I am "only temporary"? It is the Strangs who are permanent, who will go on and on like roasted vegetables in the ashes.

"Mrs. Strang, I'm Edward Glace." "Oh you are, are

you, and what do you suppose I care?" So many people start proclaiming themselves, not really knowing what it is they are proclaiming.

The fog, an extra secretion, stung his eyes. He climbed on the bus and sat downstairs on the edge of a shared seat with a notice printed on it—TO TAKE THREE PEOPLE. The other two passengers looked resentfully at him as if he were claiming more than his share of room or as if they were afraid that part of their own bodies might overflow the forbidden boundary and perhaps be stolen and never returned. Three to a seat was a dangerous practice, Edward decided. And why did Winter enlarge people? The bus was filled with women carrying baskets. The windows were shut and steamy. The bus dallied a while in a deserted space of road, with the driver and conductor making mysterious signals to each other, and once or twice the conductor alighted to visit the driver in his cabin, to exchange information and plans, communications which could not be signaled by stamping of feet, ringing of bells, or knocking and gesturing.

Edward wished he had a book to read. The woman next to him was reading a newspaper which was damp and black with morning and murder. Other passengers were talking—of weather, bargains, doctors, and treatments. Edward was not usually forced to notice the plodding rituals and confusions that composed the mass living of the human race. The closeness of people irritated him. He felt his eyes watering. He felt the pimple on his bald head stinging where he had pressed it too energetically. The women had food in their baskets, food and large flat parcels—dresses or household goods held close to their bodies, like extra limbs accidentally detached and needing care and control. A man got on the bus. He was sneezing into a large handkerchief, and when he spoke to the conductor his voice was hoarse and indistinct. He sneezed again, and the woman next to him gave him a glance of disapproval and moved away from him, to a seat up in the front of the bus. The conductor skillied the window down a few inches and a blast of cold air struck Edward on the top of his head. He moved to another seat, nearer the door. So this was humanity—tension, disagreement, discomfort, the common cold. Well why didn't I hire a taxi? Edward asked himself. He knew the answer. Humanity tempted him, in spite of its revoltingly persistent attempts to play at being pigs instead of people. It'll recover, he thought. It's just a play impulse. One day in the future it will all be changed, myself too, and humanity will find its real treasure, and men will help one another in finding it, like those wonderful birds which stand on the seashore in groups and slowly turn over the stones to find their food, their treasure: helping one another in the task, no longer jabbing their vicious beaks at their fellows' flesh;

only levering and turning the stones with their former instrument of death. . . .

"Start with man and wife, Edward," a voice said to him. "Could not you and Vera together have turned the stone of being? The seashore is a lonely place, Edward. And Edward, do you keep saying In the future, In the future, because you believe it or because you are only putting off the effort required of you to turn the stone yourself?"

"Impertinence!" Edward said aloud. He had never been spoken to before by a voice from the air. He would have to consider the meaning of it, and the danger, when he returned from the funeral.

"Impertinence!"

"Yes," the woman next to him answered. "He ought to be in bed at home, not spreading his germs in enclosed places like buses."

There is no reason to suppose, Edward kept telling himself, that my first meeting with the Strang family to mourn the death of one of them will be an historic occasion. The apprehension I have felt since I got off that terrible bus and turned the corner here into Prudence Avenue is quite a natural feeling. I have pried into their secrets, their crimes, their history, read their letters and news of them in old papers; I have copies of birth and marriage certificates. In a manner of speaking, I am their keeper; which means that they will resent and

130

despise me. What right have I to attend Lyndon Strang's funeral and mourn the man I never heard speak or laugh or weep? Yet I mourn the past dead whose lives are wedged between the great cleft of centuries I never knew. I never heard, save in my mind, the past dead speak or laugh or weep. Perhaps my visit here will give sudden meaning and clarity to all my years of research. . . .

The front door had a knocker and a bell. Edward rang the bell and listened as its urgency sprang through the corridor and into the rooms of the house, which was stuck to all the other houses in the street with that special glue which is the pride of England, and is manufactured somewhere in Scotland in a caldron on a heath in thunder and lightning. A television aerial was poised from the roof, like a new kind of flag deprived of its drapery either because the color and motto were undecided or because the object of loyalty was vanished or dead or had never existed. A group of gray pigeons drooled and waddled in the spouting on the edge of the slate roof, muttering like makeshift witches into the dirty milk jug of increasing fog, *Fail-curdle, Fail-curdle*, while the sharp-eyed rooks from their roost near the chimney flapped their rough wings of sooty stone, and cried, *Flaw, Flaw, Flaw!*

Edward rang the bell again. He heard a sound of moving furniture, footsteps, and the door opened and a slight woman with a colored handkerchief or scarf tied around her head appeared in the doorway. Beyond her he could see a bare corridor, the carpet rolled up, and a heavy table on its side at the end of the corridor.

The woman saw his glance.

"Yes, we're in a muddle," she said.

She waited for Edward to explain his visit, and stared cautiously at the area surrounding him, that is at the area of a person where mines are laid and approaches must be made with care, for some clue to his trade or to any danger which he might carry with him in bags, suitcases, boxes. She caught sight of his briefcase and frowned.

Edward smiled. "I'd like to speak to Mrs. Georgina Strang, if I may."

"Yes? I'm Mrs. Strang."

It was difficult.

"I'm Edward Glace."

"Oh?"

Edward decided to adopt an official air. He withdrew the letter from his briefcase. He smiled in what he hoped was a reassuring and friendly manner while he tried to control the anger which surged through him, Do you mean to say that I gave up my wife and child, that I spent years in musty libraries—for you? Are *you* humanity?

Edward smiled again.

Mrs. Strang frowned. "I'm busy," she said. "As you

can see I'm busy. I don't want any free offers. I don't want my house vacuum-cleaned free without obligation. I don't want to join a credit club to get my dream wardrobe. And I always vary my brand of toilet paper, week in week out. I vary my brand of everything. I've had market-research people before and I know how to deal with them."

Edward did not reply but held out the letter, which Mrs. Strang took, and seeing it was addressed to her, she frowned suspiciously.

"Are you from the G.P.O.?"

She opened the letter and began to read it.

How did you know my name and who I was? And where I lived? Who are you?

"Oh, oh, I see you're one of those people . . . I should have thought Janet and her husband would have managed to get down here, they've a lad working on the farm."

Then she stopped reading and looked curiously at Edward, as if expecting to find upon him some identification mark of his occupation, a brand burned into his skin.

"You don't look like one of those people," she said. "Lyndon was buried yesterday. Cremated. They couldn't have understood my telegram. And no matter what Janet says in her letter I'm not in the habit of asking strangers to a family funeral, no matter how many famous people you've discovered among our ancestors, I suppose your briefcase here is full of the details, I suppose you've come to blackmail us, I suppose you've discovered all the black sheep too. What right have you to spy upon our family, to worm your way into our confidence and try to uncover our secrets? I suppose you think that case at the Old Bailey was something to do with us. Let me tell you Wallace Strang is no relation to us and I know what I'd do if I were the Home Secretary and had to consider his appeal."

In her rising excitement she became voluble.

"Grass is for growing, windows are for cleaning, and murderers are for hanging," she almost shouted, at the same time seeming surprised at her outburst and frowning as if she could not understand the significance of it and the connection which had sprung suddenly in her mind between grass, windows, and murderers.

Edward spoke calmly.

"I'm terribly sorry," he said. "I expected this. I know it's rather unusual, perhaps impertinent, for me to come here intruding, and though I have long wanted to meet some living members of the Strang family, it was your sister-in-law who invited me to attend the funeral. I've worked so long on my research that I feel I know you, I feel . . ."

"I know, I know, you 'somehow feel you are one of us'? Well you're not, Mr. . . ."

"Glace. Edward Glace."

"You're not one of us. You've as much right to be one of us as that market-research person who came the other day, prying into my brands of detergent and toilet paper."

As Mrs. Strang repeated the words "one of us" she seemed to find in them a personal satisfaction. One of us against the enemy. One of us.

"One of us," she said dreamily. "Who do you mean by 'us?' "

Edward leaned forward intently, and Mrs. Strang, seeing herself reflected three times in his rimless glasses, suddenly felt bewildered and strange.

"Who do you mean? You are throwing stones, Mrs. Strang, into the ocean of people and do you believe that you should decide your boundaries by the ripples you create, that you should venture no further in your definition of 'us'? Tell me, who do *you* mean by 'us?' "

Mrs. Strang looked startled. She had seen herself three times in this crank's glasses, and the sight made her dizzy and blurred the outline of things and people, and the table at the end of a corridor gave a deep groan, with cramp in its folding slide-out belly, and the very floor she stood on winced in its nakedness. It was the fault of this crank market fellow.

Mrs. Strang made as if to shut the door.

"I'm busy," she said. "I'm in mourning." As if the

135

state of mourning were one characterized by ceaseless activity.

"I don't know whatever came over Janet to write in this way and suggest you come to Lyndon's funeral. I'm glad it's over, for it would have upset me dreadfully to have a stranger turn up, you with your briefcase coming along to Honour Oak with us and staring at the coffin with goodness knows what in your head about our ancestors. I've never been much interested myself, though I know we do have distinguished people, but it's none of your business, it's absolutely none of your business. I tell you, you're no better than the market-research people wanting to know our brand of toilet paper. I fooled them. I said I didn't remember which brand I used. Then they named a few, saying on and on, Haven't you ever heard of that brand, surely you have heard of this brand? Then they came at me with another brand but all the time I said No, No, I change my brand from week to week and never remember the name. I fooled them."

Edward listened attentively, trying not to look like a market-research interviewer, a poke-nose, a crank, and all the types that she considered him to be, trying instead to look sympathetic, a little sad—after all, the funeral had been only yesterday, the family was upset, they were moving somewhere—where?—they were refugees. . . .

"I'm sorry you feel like this about my work, Mrs. Strang. I assure you that I have been very discreet in all my research dealing with your family history. I have wanted so much to meet you. You have my deepest sympathy in the death of your husband."

"Deepest sympathy! I don't suppose you know what death means!"

"Oh I do, I do," Edward assured her. "When my wife died . . ."

"You wife is dead?"

"Oh yes," Edward told her earnestly, pausing a while for her to grasp the fact and to realize the grief he must have suffered.

"I'm sorry. I didn't know. Was it sudden, like Lyndon's? Lyndon's was flu. What did your wife die of, if I'm not being inquisitive?"

"Cancer."

"Cancer! Oh Mr. Glace, it's a terrible word isn't it? Cancer. Practically everybody's dying of cancer, the whole country is riddled with it. I'm sorry Mr. Glace. Would you like a cup of tea?"

Her voice was full of concern as if Edward had only then received the news of his wife's death.

"If you care for it I'll make a cup of tea. We had arranged to move to one of the New Towns, and everything was fixed up, and then the flu came, why did he have to catch the bad flu? But I'm forgetting you and your wife, I suppose you've been through bad times since she passed on—what made you so interested in the Strangs? You believe me, don't you, when I say that Wallace Strang is no connection with us?"

Suddenly she turned and seeming to see for the first time the empty corridor, the carpet rolled up, the table lying on its side, she gave a swift cry as if something had been snatched from her.

"Just look! Moving to a New Town. They say you die a slow death when you get to a New Town. There's no rubbish in the streets, they're so clean you could eat off them, and you're forbidden to do anything, like in heaven.

"Are you a religious man, Mr. Glace? Are you a Christian? What use do you think it is with things in the world today as they are and those high up prepared to kill because they're scared to apologize, what's wrong with apologizing, it's manners, but what's the use of hymns When He Cometh When He Cometh To Make Up His Jewels when they're paste or stolen and anyway they break when you touch them. Would you like a cup of tea to help you forget your wife's death? Cancer! There's a cancer hospital not far from here, run by the nuns, and there's a morgue attached, and every day the hearse is coming and going coming and going like grocery deliveries or TV sets being called for and returned with the tube fixed at what a price and even then you have to walk the aerial round the room to get a picture. But why do you stand on the doorstep like that; come in and I'll make a cup of tea. You're one of us, Mr. Glace."

"Do you know what Death is?" Edward asked. "Is it really the TV set being called for and repaired? My wife . . ."

"Yes, your wife. Tell me about her. Are you going to publish about the Strangs in journals and newspapers? In a book? Are you writing a book about us? There's enough material in the Strang family for a whole library of books. Why did you choose us, out of all the families in the world? There's nothing special about us—here there's just myself and Molly who sits the exam this year and will go on to grammar school which is more than I did or Lyndon. But don't you think really it's awful cheek of you to come here and want to be at my husband's funeral. Just like that. As if you were entitled to it. I'm sorry about your wife but haven't you got your own family to study, you're old enough to have almost a grown-up family, and then you'll have ancestors of your own, why can't you uncover some of your own secrets, why can't you spend your time with research on the Glaces, what a strange name, something to do with ice isn't it, the Ice Age, which reminds me the winter is as bitter as we've ever had it but there's been no snow only those few dirty gray flakes at Christ-

139

mas. Now if I were going to do research into a family I'd do my own family, look up my ancestors, make lists, a family tree, leaves, blossoms, and the time . . ."

". . . the time it was struck by lightning which killed all who sheltered under it, beasts and men."

"What do you mean, killed by lightning? Isn't it dark this morning? With the door open the fog's coming in and down my throat; it collects, doesn't it, everywhere it goes it collects. I was going to put a notice in the local paper No Flowers By Request, Donations to . . . but I couldn't have said Donations to the Influenza Research Fund, could I, it would have seemed a letdown, yet it's common, the flu, but it would have made a joke of Lyndon's death to have put about it in the paper, you know, aspirin and lemon drinks and a sniffly nose, but if it had been cancer or one of those interesting blood diseases—there are more of them now aren't there, with radiation and the like—or if it had been the heart it would have sounded important and serious, it's terrible isn't it the way things which are serious can get to sound like a joke even if it means you die of them; so I had them send flowers instead of a donation. My husband's like the invisible man, and my excuse for going on like this is that I saw myself three times in your glasses—are they contact lenses? To tell you the truth I use the same brand of toilet paper year in year out, it's the brand that the advertisements say the doctors use and doctors must

140

know because they've got the inside information about germs; yes to tell you the truth I'm glad he's dead. He drank. Even when he was dead there was a stink of beer, and they were so good at the crematorium they put all kinds of holy funeral smells to try and cover it up and arranged the flowers carefully but flowers these days don't have scent, they're all indoors or hothouse or plastic so lifelike you can't believe your eyes, but whether it was in my mind or not I could smell the beer all the time, even in the ashes; they were ashes like after a picnic or a fire on a bomb site where they burn old motor tires and broken bedsteads. . . ."

Then suddenly Mrs. Strang turned fiercely upon Edward who was still standing at the door while the fog swirled about them, filling the corridor where Georgina Strang was standing, "And if you really want to know, the chap at the Old Bailey, the murderer, is our first cousin. There. What's the use of hushing it up? I suppose you'll call on him now before he is hanged and tell him about his wonderful ancestors and show him the family tree with the beetles in the bark and the maggots in the pulp. It's time we all died. I don't know what's come over me. It's time we all died, coughing and sneezing and sniffing up our nose those green tubes like tiny rockets to deaden everything in our heads. I used to think everything would be wonderful, with a clear beginning and end and me wearing a floral dress in the sun with white clouds in the sky and the stones white and clean on the pavement, and people passing with light all frothing round them like clouds and in bed making love dissolving like a river running over pebbles and Lyndon terribly strong and supporting like timber with dark whirling knots in his eyes and that brown seasoned smell like a forest. . . . Are you a market-research interviewer or the Minister of Communications?"

She banged the door shut.

Edward stood, undecided, holding his briefcase, the letter to Georgina Strang still in his hand. He looked at his watch. He had been standing there for ten minutes, imagining his interview with Georgina Strang. He had not even dared to ring the doorbell loud enough for it to be heard and answered. He wished that he had not accepted the invitation to the funeral. He wished that he had never ventured to get in touch with the living Strangs. Couldn't he just ride by the Present with his eyes closed and reach the future and potter about the seashore among the wonderful turnstones . . . He rang the bell. The door opened and a small dark woman appeared.

"Yes?"

"I'm Edward Glace. You may have heard of me from your sister Janet. I have a letter from her."

"Oh yes. Do come in Mr. Glace. We are very flattered to hear of your interest in our family."

There was a pause while she read the letter.

"As a matter of fact I've just got back from the funeral. It was early. The undertakers are busy these days."

Edward found it hard to discern evidence of her grief.

"We have to take death in our stride," she said. "Lyndon has been ill for a long time, off and on. What exactly do you want to know about the family, Mr. Glace?"

"Nothing at the moment," Edward replied. "One has to have time to recover from one's grief, hasn't one?"

"One?"

She seemed to be seized by a mood of jealousy and possessiveness.

"One? It's *my* grief, there's no question of 'one' this and 'one' that."

"Of course you're right."

She nodded vaguely.

"I'm sorry you missed the funeral. I'm rather busy now, but anything you want to know I'll be glad to tell you. My little girl's staying with friends for the day. You'll have to meet her. She's a Strang, a real Strang. What made you take up the Strang family?"

Edward never knew what to reply to this question. "I was interested," he said. "Deeply interested."

She seemed satisfied.

"Yes," she said, "we *are* an interesting family. I always knew we were not all that ordinary and common. It's an old family, isn't it? It goes back, doesn't it?"

Edward assured her that it was old and that it went back.

She did not inquire into its future or whether it had any future.

"If you don't mind," she said, "I was going out when you called. I can't spend the day by myself, and I'm going to friends for a few days."

She held out her hand. The nails were chipped and pink with polish.

"Pleased to have met you, indeed."

He saw that she had been crying. He wondered when she had chosen to indulge her grief. She seemed the kind of person who could say, I will cry now, I will laugh now, and who would prepare her surroundings carefully, removing the boiling kettle from the gas, locking the back door, turning off the television, even washing the dishes and sweeping the room, before she could enjoy her outburst. Or perhaps she had cried during the night between two and three o'clock in that silence which occurs when all the car doors in the street have been slammed and the visitors have gone home, and the record players have been switched off, and the covered lorries (he had noticed one in the street as he arrived) drowsed in a quiet corner before being set to throb and choke an hour or so later; between two and three o'clock Georgina Strang had wept in the ordinary way, sniffing, and looking for her handkerchief, and switching on the light in order to see clearly under the pillow and amongst the bedclothes, soaking her handkerchief, dampening her pillow, weeping first because of a quarrel she had years ago with Lyndon and never said she was sorry, and then weeping because she would be all alone in bed with no skin to touch except her own, and no one to talk to, to say, "Listen," to or "Did you know what," to; crying for her sad lot and that of her daughter left alone without a father, and then crying without pretense for the last and first reason—crying because she herself would die in the end, and no one would be able to tell her when or how, not that she wanted to know, but simply that no one would warn her and it would come suddenly, even then without her recognizing it, and she could never bear to have secrets kept from her, to be taken in by disguises. . . .

"It's a pleasure to have met you," Edward said, shaking hands with her. "And if you're interested and want to know anything further about your family history I'm always ready to help."

"That's so kind of you," she said, taking his card.

E. Glace,

Genealogist.

"Fancy, just fancy that you should find so much to study in our family history! My sister says you have spent years on it. It must be like the history of the world!"

"It *is* the history of the world."

She drew her hands across her narrow bosom in a gesture of conserving suddenly acquired wealth which was in some way connected with herself as a person, a wife, a mother, and now a widow. A slight color appeared in her pale cheeks. She laughed on an excited note.

"Who would have thought it?" she exclaimed. "If Lyndon had known . . . that we were like the history of the world . . . perhaps he would have been angry. I'm sure he would have been angry. Yet he always said his family was so important, that he had to carry on the line, and I used to laugh because I always kept thinking of firemen, a long line of them, you know the way they pass buckets of water one to the other to put out the fire! And I said, it's all right continuing the line if you know what you're carrying and what you're trying to kill in the end.

"Good-bye then Mr. Glace. And thank you so much. Oh . . . oh . . . there's that affair of Wallace Strang, the murderer. Of course he is no connection with us, no connection at all. Thank you then Mr. Glace."

"It was nothing," Edward muttered, suddenly bashful as if he had performed an act of chivalry in public.

He felt ashamed and depressed as Georgina Strang, adjusting her former pale mask, shut the door and left him standing feeling useless, on her doorstep.

So that was the Strang family, he thought angrily, saying to himself, Well? Well? What did you expect? It does not seem that in this generation we shall admit that we are murderers; in the future it may be too late. . . .

Georgina Strang had reminded him of his wife, of Vera, yet there was little resemblance between them; yet every woman reminded him of his wife, there seemed to be a secret likeness between all people, as if some borrowed the characteristics of others, for a day or two, or kept them for life and for death, as if between the entire human race there was this constant invisible exchanging and bargaining, transmitting of smiles and whims and gestures, in an attempt to efface all individual identity, to escape from the responsibility of owning unique essence and a name.

"A network of deceit," Edward said. "We can't stand alone. We have to be imitating, bargaining, transacting every part of ourselves. Why should Vera aspire to be Georgina Strang?" But it was this fluidity of people which fascinated him. No river reaches the sea unless it flows. The dream of Edward's life was the time when the human race would reach the sea, when it would not be important who was Georgina Strang and who was Vera Glace, or who was anybody, there would be no Strang family, no names, and none of the guilt arising from the denial of essence and name. . . .

Galleons, old caves where the drowned look in windows with the weed floating across their eyes, the dead kept under by the hand of the water, which moves softly, powerfully, and how the parched dead spring to the surface, light, white merry bones which form a rocking chair for the sun to laze in and pay the rent to the landlord dead, the invisible flesh changed into salt and shells and singing fish . . .

"You have a curious life, Edward," the voice said to him. "You are a child playing hopscotch with your life, stepping within the boundaries, making your own chalk circles, while in the next street in the next town, in the next mind and being, other circles are being drawn which bear no correspondence to the ones you make. And all the Strang family have signed their initials in your boundaries. What does that mean, Edward? Is not your life curious?"

Edward smiled dreamily.

"It is indeed, but I have never heard voices before. When I get home on this terrible bus I shall consider the fact of you, of this voice in my ear. Meanwhile I have railway engines in my eyes, going uphill, and sending smoke all over me, over my best suit, my shoes, my body, my face, and my bald head."

"The Strangs, the Strangs, the Strangs," the voice said.

"In rhythm," Edward replied, and his heart felt heavy as he boarded the terrible bus.

10

I have heard from Edward. He seems confused. He mentions a voice addressing him eight inches from his left ear. He has been extravagant, he says, and bought himself a new teapot which withholds the tea leaves like vital information from the gossipy bowl of his teacup. Yet he seems to have been elevated by a sudden leverage of his entire mind, as if he had been thrust into an upstairs view with direct access to the upper level of people's minds where the nests of ideas are built and the younkers hatch out gawky and shivering and nobbly fleshed with their shovel-mouths wide to the sky, scooping the essence of light and the tidbits dropped from the close fierce bulk of their Faithful Protector; their hide-and-seek God.

I have not yet had time to consider the fact that this is my first news of Edward for many years. I wonder if in middle age he has enough breath to inflate the life jacket to throw out to his drowning humanity? Strange that I remember how he used to warn me when I somehow got the habit of babbling on and on, at breakfast, while he sat silent, "Save your breath, save your breath," when all the time he was secretly filling envelopes and pockets bottles and boxes with his own breathing, for use later when a pain comes over the heart, and ladders, stairs, paths to the sky have to be labored up, with a tense white face and the mouth grabbing at the lordly charity of breath.

Erlene must speak, Edward urges in his letter. Erlene must speak. His desire for a significant message from his daughter (the last words he heard her say were, if I remember that little piece she stood up to recite for him before he went away,

> Old Meg she was a gipsy
> and lived upon the moors,
> her bed it was the brown heath turf,
> her house was out of doors. . . .)

and his interest in a member of the Strang family living in Dunedin have prompted him to decide. He is flying here from London. I never knew that his paper-and-paste wings could be so surely relied upon to carry him over so many miles of ocean where the sharks wait, clear-headed, for his blood to trickle down the walls of the sky. He's taking a risk of course; as long as he gets enough breath up there so close to the sun and the sky. Oh why have we never been like all the others in accepting each day in black and white without question or scrutiny? There would have been something like happiness, for Edward, myself, Erlene, perhaps other children, had we not taken our magnifying glass and discovered

150

the currency of time to be counterfeit. It happened only because somewhere at a certain moment one of us by chance picked up a genuine coin, judged it to be genuine, and thus could never recall the judgment. So the shining vision stays, expands, takes up room. The tiny threepenny truth melts and flows and silvers the entire view and runs down the edge of being, like moonlight; and all the time with the silver vision before us we judge, judge. I am alone always now. What is the use of chanting the jingle, Husband, wife, child, Edward, Vera, Erlene, of putting ourselves in the togetherness pose of the advertisements, arm-in-arm before the radio or washing machine, with polishings of love on our faces, and exclamations, confidences, bursting like frozen green peas from our fur-lined pod heads? It is nothing like that. All that remains of our lives is the ceaseless useless effort to find the instrument which will saw through the bars, the mile-wide walls; or to tunnel under and emerge, gasping for air, smeared like beasts with our own dung, and then only to be turned away as strangers from ourselves and from others.

I am innocent, surely I am innocent. Yet even when I make an apple pie and press my thumb around the edge of the golden crust, when the time comes for eating it I am swallowing apple pie and thumb prints, crisp guilt topped with cream! Edward seems to think that Erlene will open her mouth and pronounce like an oracle; *I* know that the first words she utters will be a statement of my guilt, a judgment upon me. But she still does not speak. She visits the doctor once or twice in ten days, and when she comes home she takes her place by the window and spends the time peering at the insects on the sill as if the source of her hope for the future lay not in human beings but in a ladybird, a blackbeetle, a blowfly with his undercarriage packed with death. I don't know what she dreams or thinks about. She eats, she sleeps, she walks with me to the shops for occasional messages; she reads —never library books, but only those on her shelves. She seems so infuriatingly self-contained as if there were never any need to speak, as if human speech were merely a bad habit, like war, politics, religion, picked up in the course of history with the leisurely aim of disposing of, entertaining, or calming the human race; as if we could have managed very well with or even without the first few grunts and cries which survival has given publicity to, and gratitude has enlarged, and love has touched and shaped and offered a share of life, accepting death and nothingness in exchange. Is speech no more than a comfortable, satisfying habit?

My curiosity about Erlene is even more intense than my sympathy and my desire for her to get well. If only I could find out quickly, before it is too late, what thoughts are in her head, what rows and borders of thoughts in neat bud but never bursting to speech. Ed-

152

ward is right. I understand his urgency. She must speak. If she does not speak I am doomed, Edward is doomed—he and his magic ring of Strangs (he wears the private life belt which he dreams of throwing to the human race)—the whole world is doomed because it will seem to have accepted the silence which lurks beyond and within us, only waiting for us to surrender. Edward is right again. We cannot surrender. Over these millions of years we have built up diplomatic ties with silence, signing treaties, exchanging information, encouraging tourist trade on this and the other side of silence and darkness; there has been peace between us, although through these millions of years the enemy has been lying in wait—and what of the bodies carried away over the border at dead of night, the marauding dreams, the ceaseless sabotage of silence? We cannot withdraw now, and stop speaking. Erlene, and all others who are mute, must learn to speak, not mere animal cries, demands for food, warmth, love, nor human pleas for forgiveness salvation peace of mind, but the speech which arranges the dance and pattern of the most complicated ideas and feelings of man in relation to truth; truth; it, the center; the circus, the crack of the whip, the feeding time of the spirit; then the great striped tigers leaping unharmed through the fire. It is something to hope for.

But in the next room—silence always. Dr. Clapper believes that soon Erlene may utter something. He too seems to be infected with this curiosity, almost with fear, when confronted by Erlene. And I? I suppose I am only waiting to die forgiven. I was never a Brownie or a Girl Guide. In those blue and green companies of people they learn to tie knots in the belief that knots are important. Neat books of rules, words underlined, lists of duties to be performed, perfect training for the life of a man or woman; all the so beautiful knots tied, and badges awarded for the ability to tie them.

Blue and green companies of people tying knots and exposed to silence.

Also lighting fires, but fires that could be controlled by an imperious breath or a lash of the hand; not these fires of speech which refuse to die, smoldering and spreading no matter how much the silence is heaped upon them.

When I take Erlene to the hospital tomorrow I shall explain that her father will soon be visiting New Zealand, that he is anxious for Erlene to speak and that he believes he may be able to help her. We are all afflicted with these notions of our own power. Erlene can very well go to the hospital by herself yet I go with her, striding by her as if to tell the world, This is Erlene Glace who cannot speak. Secretly, she cannot walk either. Don't you see how she relies upon me, her mother, to help her walk to the hospital? See how unselfishly I lend her my power of movement! Soon it is my influence which will make her speak, and when she does speak I want you to know that

I, I only, have been responsible for her recovery. Recovery?

I cannot convince myself that silence is an affliction; perhaps after all, I am in league with the enemy.

Well soon Edward will be flying in (who has repaired his paper-and-paste wings? A woman, certainly.) He will rush to Erlene, stare at her wildly with his dark eyes, and wait confidently for her to speak—because he is her father, because he is near her and possesses the power to inspire her to speech. His dark hair will fall over his forehead as he makes his energetic listening movements, for I remember he was inclined to listen with his body and with movements of his head as if sound were an object, a visible blow, to be parried, received, rejected, attacked. What a tight wadding of memory I have wound about my Edward in order to protect him (and me), in my mind at least, from the stain and mildew fertilized and set in growth by this perpetual downpour of time. I keep forgetting that Time leaks through. I do not know Edward. I shall not know him when I unwrap the shawl of memory and consider the rotting perceptions hoarded over so many years. He and I shall never again be lovers. This town is my lover, this house, this land; these provide an area, an accommodation of love which human beings have never been able to give me or which, lacking the constructive ability, I have never been able to build for myself from cut and measured blocks of flesh and blood.

155

I am happy enough to open myself under the sun, to permit the intimacies of weather, even to whispering at first the conventional troubled, Stop it, not now, to a determined wind coming in hungry and warm from the Canterbury plains, having spent the previous night in a bed of snow somewhere in the Southern Alps. I have no questions to ask the weather, the sun and sky and the wind and rain; I do not wander over the hills, jealously tugging at sleeves of cloud, with poetic cross-examination, "Have you seen the wind?" searching in bush and tussock and snow grass for the wayward gallivanting southerly or in the gum trees for the hot-headed nor'-wester. The storm and rain and sun and wind come and go as they please; I have no suspicions, no demands for declarations of love.

Yet as part of my solitary way of life I also have a silent daughter and the memory of a husband who keeps people, like hens or pigs, in an enclosure of Time, hoping to protect them from extinction; he feeds and fattens their histories; all has been well; only now they have strayed into the present—how will he cope with them? His letter says very little, yet why should I expect him to confide in me? The affair of a voice in his left ear is troubling, and a cause for jealousy on my part, for I know that the air is full of voices speaking to us, uttering platitudes and wise sayings, yet so few of us have the knack of switching on to this extra source of information, amusement, inspiration, annoyance, and fear. I can't help asking why Edward should profit from these voices when most of us hear nothing but silence in the air around us, since we do not possess that magnet which draws sound in its tantalizingly devious journey from our own heads, out into the air, and then, refreshed and enriched, back into our own ears.

It will be winter when Edward arrives. At the moment as I gaze out at the leftover summer and the torn circus-hangings of autumn, I am fit only for dreaming. Already the memory of the sheen of crocuses down on the flat near the creek has sunk deep to be replaced by all these damp swirling leaves with their individual flurries and personal panics, caught suddenly in passing currents of death; the hissing rain like an arched gray cat cornered by the enemy and striking out with its poisonous claws; the cream-and-green moss lying soft, bubbled with rain, along the apple branches; the sodden squelched earth. The town baths are closed for the season. The bay is deserted, the ice-cream shop and the restaurant are closed, the merry-go-rounds seem faded and rusted, as if the truth will out, concealed for so many months by the deceptions of summer. The excursion trains running between here and north and south have ceased, and the express trains passing on the railway line opposite the house have all their windows shut, the glass misted, sheltering the passengers from the approaching damp and dark of winter. Down in the park the leaves have fallen and been swept, and all the white and blue and red flags that marked the circuit for running and jumping and relays have been pulled up and stored away, and the little holes in the ground where they stood flapping merrily in the wind are filled with rainwater, and on the worn grass the footprints of the swift and the strong have changed to hollows, like hoofprints, patterned containers for mud and rain; and over to the left of the park, near the town creek that slinks in a green slime over the artificial waterfall, the earth is still churned with the muddy memory of the last circus.

I see by the evening paper that the Little Theatre Society is rehearsing a new play, that a lecturer from the University Adult Education Department is conducting a series of lectures on modern art, in that little room above the Public Library; that the Caledonian Club is busy once more with meetings, elections, entertainments; that more dances are being arranged, indoor basketball clubs are holding annual meetings, entrance forms have been issued for the yearly competitions to be held in the winter holidays in the Opera House; that all the summer societies have presented their annual reports and balance sheets—the rowing and swimming and yachting clubs.

Few caravans remain, down in the motor camp. The paddocks are not filled with visitors from the North and South wanting to see the Old Mill or count the fish in the creek or to stand on top of the hill while the motorcycle rally roars through the open country roads. The town is growing more quiet and still. All is in order. Winter will soon be here, not the panic-stricken darkness of the northern hemisphere, that inevitable slow approach of doom where each human being is forced to become a valiant Atlas shouldering his burden of sky, but a more optimistic southern season where a remote light plays about the upper sky, as watch light and guardian of the absent summer. In this land there is no real clamping down of death, no sealed room of darkness, only a kind of seasonal tent with the edges flapping to admit the light and one or two occasional playful days trying to touch the green canvas for the lost warm spring rain to strike through and tug out of bed, too early, the first crocuses in green and gold swank and shine. Here in the southern hemisphere we realize the humor of death, the tricks it plays, the need not to take it too seriously when we find it standing near throwing stones into the darkness—the need to remember to believe that the stones are not people, that human fantasy also plays tricks when it gazes down to the dim shapes of moss- and lichen-grown bodies falling so fast through the darkness. In the northern hemisphere we say without questioning—Those stones are people dying. But here in the south we laugh and remind ourselves, Stones are stones, the nightmare is the nightmare and not the reality.

Or so we like to believe, and the sun is on our side, pampering us with too much light dripped down to our quiescent minds and bodies from its golden medicine spoon.

And Edward will travel from winter to winter. Why does he hear voices? It is said to be a sign of madness, but what is madness but a vivid glimpse into the human factory where the limbs are pasted to the body and the attitudes stapled in the head, and the self labeled—all long before the inspection which decides the "perfects," the "substandard," the "rejects." Madness is only Open Day in the factory of the mind. We can walk through, prodding and touching, questioning, feeling wonder at the innumerable patterns of strangeness which woven and processed, parceled and delivered, bear no resemblance to the original materials, yet contain them and are part of them.

Is Edward mad, then? Or is he a reject running in and out of the single file of Strangs?

Sometimes I feel that when I move through my life I am lashed to the deck, wax is set in my ears, in order that I too may not be lured to destruction by the noise of humanity. Has Edward decided to accept the terrible commotion? Does Erlene speak to me and am I so afraid of death that I cannot hear?

Presently, I shall know. Edward is certain she will speak to him. I hope that his wings have been thoroughly inspected in the factory, that he does not fly too close to the sun, that when he is alone over the ocean he is not tempted to change to a seabird, discarding human speech for the limited perpetual cry of yearning which gets seabirds and men nowhere unless it is strained, poured, molded and set in words, those solid little bombs that in one explosion can free a prisonful of pities, and set them working—as angels making mailbags to carry the messages.

11

Erlene wished that her mother would not talk so much when they were going to the hospital. They always went up the back way now, through the fence by the frog pond, up the hill past the broom bushes that had determinedly spat out their brown seeds and by the gorse with the autumn spider webs strung between the dry spikes, along by the Nurses' Home and the laundry, and one or two rich people's houses with their two stories and the passion fruit around the doorway and the shrubs cut to beast-size in the garden, and then to the hospital, along the brown polished corridors with the hospital smell which had no relation to people who were being persuaded to speak but was concerned only with bodies, broken legs, appendicitis, tonsils, fevers, and operating rooms.

As soon as Erlene and her mother came to the room where Dr. Clapper was waiting, the smell which had accompanied them along the corridor suddenly vanished as if to say, This part of the hospital is not my affair, I am related to splints and bandages and plaster and medicines, I have no interest in girls who do not speak because they are unable to think or because there is nothing left to say

162

or because there are no words or whatever the reason, and anyway I have nothing to do with girls who sit and talk to Uncle Blackbeetle when they should be getting ready to leave school and take their places in the world, which does not revolve, don't you believe it, but is fixed with a drawing pin and the places are decided for you and you stand in them, as in stables, with your head poking out and turning this way and that when the man carrying the food walks past at a certain hour each day until you are dead. This I know. I am a smell, a hospital smell, clean and paid for, and thank goodness I am made of different substance from people. No, Erlene, I cannot accompany you to this part of the hospital, I must retreat to my own quarters and frolic amongst the broken bodies and the toppling temperatures; I am no escort for minds or speech or hearing or sight. I am an escort for bodies, chiefly for limbs, which do very well the way they hold together without glue.

Erlene's mother kept talking. On and on. Erlene, she was saying. Erlene, look down over the harbor, can you see that little ship out there against the horizon, just think to what strange countries it has voyaged. Can you see there, by the breakers, by the stone wall, where there used to be land and now there is sea; erosion, Erlene; the land is being drawn under, sucked under by the sea. Oh, an aeroplane, look! See, out the country, spraying fertilizer. Oh the leaves in the Gardens! That empty house,

163

gouged-out eyes, an old old story but the air is full of spikes. The sun, Erlene!

Then her mother would sigh.

"All these things to see and you won't talk to me about them! But perhaps you're right, perhaps there's nothing to say! Yet I can't let myself believe that, Erlene. Don't you understand that for the sake of survival we can't just throw away our language as if it were an empty ice-cream carton!"

"I wonder what Dr. Clapper will talk about today, my dear." Her mother always sighed and wondered what Dr. Clapper would say to her. When the interview was over her mother always seemed to be waiting for information.

"Tell me," she would entreat. "Do tell me, Erlene!"

They walked in the grass and her mother worried because their ankles got wet.

"Our ankles are wet in the long grass," she said. It sounded like doom. "Our ankles are wet."

Why was everything so strange that wet ankles became a kind of doom? What relation had they to Death? Was everything in relation, intertwined with tiny wires that shocked you when you touched them?

But the hospital smell was aloof. "Good-bye," it said, as Erlene and her mother approached Dr. Clapper's office. "Good-bye, I am going no further, here is my boundary."

It gave a bandagy sniff and retreated leaving Erlene's

164

mother gazing about her as if she had arrived on a new planet which had no safe fence around it, for when Erlene walked alone toward the door, her mother suddenly thrust her arms forward as if to protect Erlene from falling, but how could she contain her in her extended arms and hands with their lacey gloves, fish-net design with salt water flowing and gold coins dropping through the holes; a handful of people would tangle, Erlene knew, in her mother's arms, there was no safety with so many outlets for notions fantasies and feelings that could not always be block-packaged into a size which could take care of itself in the perforated world where the darkness rushed below like water and whirl-pools.

Dr. Clapper opened the door. For a moment Erlene imagined that he reached forward and took her evening cape from her shoulders, and murmured, "I heard your foot on the stair, my dear." But all he said was, "Ah."

He said it again, and smiled. "Ah."

It seemed that he and Erlene were still old friends.

"Ah, old thing!"

Her mother frowned, then managed and molded to polite size the smile which began at her lips and finished, sadly, on the brink of her dark eyes. Her mother was wearing a brown costume of thick, compressed material, flecked with gold; the color of dates, bulky, with the bits

of stone and grit and yellow dessert not yet removed and
no tiny fork, for convenience, to taste them.

"Good morning Dr. Clapper," her mother said.

(See how polite my daughter would be, if she could
speak! See how well I am speaking for her, Dr. Clapper!
Invite me in and speak to me and let me speak, to show
how neatly I arrange the words!)

His pants were so fashionable, tight, like minstrel's
pants, his tie was splashed with black circles, and his
collar sat in a firm V, prodding his neck. He sat facing
Erlene in the room which she was beginning to know
well—she realized that the corners and walls were her
friends, but the door and window had proved themselves
to be deceitful with unexpected comings and goings and
mirrors and handkerchiefs of light waving at the trans-
fixed crowd gaping at the sun; and there were certain
areas of the room which remained foreign and refused to
learn the language or to invite Erlene to enter and be
friends—these were the two corners behind Dr. Clapper,
and the space and the floor beyond his desk. Dr. Clapper
had control of the window and the switchboard which
received the signals of light and the cries of passing birds.
In the top right-hand corner of the pane there was a
squashed fly with dried rays of spurted blood, bright red,
spreading from it. The blood should be darker, Erlene
thought. Flies' blood is dark raspberry. But it is nearly

166

winter and soon the flies will be gone away therefore perhaps they need cherry-red blood. I never speak to anyone. I haven't spoken for many many years.

"We're going to tell each other secrets, aren't we?"

She thought for a moment that he would put out his hand and say, "Tickle my hand and if I smile, you know, if I smile . . ." and that he would quote the rhyme,

> Can you keep a secret,
> I don't believe you can,
> You must not laugh,
> You must not cry,
> But do the best you can.

But his face was stern behind his smile. They were enemies. There were no promises, no rewards. He had killed the fly with his morning newspaper, and he had said to himself,

> Little fly, thy summer's play,
> my thoughtless hand has brushed away,

reciting through the poem until he made the reckless confession which so frightened him that he was devoting half his mind (sliced and measured) to trying to withdraw the words,

Then am I a happy fly,
If I live or if I die.

At the same time, though he was preoccupied with his slaughter of the fly, he made it clear that he was completely in charge of the window and that as a concession he would let her control the door. How cunning he was! He did not declare hostilities, oh no, there was no parade of weapons and threats, but it was easy to see that he was lying in wait for the kill.

He smiled and smiled.

"My head is full of things to say to you," he said. "Why, Erlene, I have so many things to talk about!"

She stared at him; she was prepared to acknowledge his accumulating store of things to say; and to marvel at them, if he wished.

"So many things to say," he kept repeating, at last forgetting to smile so that his expression was sad, as if he had arrived at the truth: his head was empty, the wind whistled in the spare rooms between the walls and the torn wallpaper and under the threadbare carpet, moaned in the corridors and around the house in and out the broken windows, looking for news, and there was no news.

There is nothing to say, Erlene thought. The house is empty, there is no one at home.

"Your mother tells me that you like to sit by the window and look at the insects on the windowsill. I often feel that insects are more exciting than people—don't you? What a time one can spend studying them, learning from them! He spoke as if he particularly wanted Erlene to know that every day as soon as he finished work he sat by the windowsill in his house, looking at the insects; that if he had no work to do he would spend all his time with the insects.

"Insects are marvelous," he exclaimed, scraping his hands over his desk as if raking a little pile of treasure toward him.

"Marvelous! They're a whole world, a whole new world!"

He was advertising. She had bought the product on her own, without reading the advertisements; she did not see why he should divide himself into blue and gold and green squares with outsize lettering merely to put across the attractions of Uncle Blackbeetle.

Dr. Clapper smiled, and the smile stayed a long time on his face, changing itself from a pale crease to a cooked golden mellow smile; and suddenly Erlene put her hand in the oven, burned her fingers, and returned his smile.

Calmly he adjusted his writing paper on the desk before him, picked up the hospital pen with its crippled nib and bellyful of dust, which hospital nibs eat, to keep alive and the situation under control, and ran his finger along the edge of the pen, as if looking for thorns.

"I understand how you feel, Erlene," he said. "I feel the same way."

He was safe, just this side of a lie, and he knew it, and it gave him the confidence to smile again in such a way that Erlene returned his smile, she could not help it.

Again calmly he adjusted his writing paper and smoothed the hospital pen, but Erlene was not watching him anymore, she was away in a field full of poppies with a legend of death kept practical by an array of speaking tombstones and a cipher; night, and then day, and the scratched face of sunlight emerging from the tomcat ecstasies of night.

"She is improving," Dr. Clapper said, when he spoke to her mother. "Soon she may be speaking. And if, as you say, her father is making a visit to New Zealand, that may be the event which finally prompts her to speak."

Then Dr. Clapper looked nervous. Erlene was watching him, and listening. He looked secretively about him.

"What manner of man is he, again, her father?"

And so, she said to Uncle Blackbeetle, I sat there and simply laughed and laughed. What manner of man is he again her father! Such a jumble of words, as if my father were a man again and again. I say Persevere, don't you, Uncle Blackbeetle? I say, Wait until the world is silent and dark and then knock and do not wait for the reply, but enter, even if you have to smash the door; but wait for silence.

Uncle Blackbeetle did not answer. Erlene had noticed that since her visits to Dr. Clapper Uncle Blackbeetle had been more than usually preoccupied with his own affairs and seldom bothered to reply to her, and often it seemed as if he had not heard what she was telling him. Surely it cannot mean that our language is changing? she wondered, in panic. Then she thought, No, there are so many coffins to prepare, it is understood that he cannot afford the time to listen or to talk.

"Talk to me, Uncle Blackbeetle," she pleaded. "Are you like Dr. Clapper, with your head full of stories?"

And then everything was all right and Erlene was not lonely anymore, and it did not seem as if the language between her and Uncle Blackbeetle was changing, for Uncle Blackbeetle once again took off his black apron (he could not tell stories while he was wearing his apron) and sat on the tiny stool which he had fashioned from twisted stalks of tinkertailor with a bright cushion of dahlia petals.

"I'll tell you a story," he said.

"About the soldiers in twos and threes?"

"No."

"About the hawks and the people speckled with death?"

"No."

"Is it Death then?"

Uncle Blackbeetle looked offended.

"Of course it is Death," he said. "What else is there to tell stories about? Did you never learn, when working fractions, to find the common denominator?"

"I am a woman," Erlene replied. "I was going to leave school and take my place in the world. One day the teacher said, 'Right, right! Now what are you all going to be?' And some were going to be nurses, others to be teachers, housewives, doctors, telephonists, to work in shops, offices; and everybody spoke up so sharply and swiftly—for when you are asked questions like this you always *speak up*, you never just *speak* otherwise the world will not hear you and prepare itself to greet you and place the traps and nets in the suitable places; so everybody spoke up and everything was so wonderfully neat and audible, and afterward, to clinch the cause and meaning of our lives, the teacher said again, this time in a triumphant manner, 'Right. Right!' Now you tell me, Uncle Blackbeetle, what was the common denominator of that fraction?"

"Riddles," said Uncle Blackbeetle. "The common denominator of all fractions is Death. But I do not know of schoolgirls, my stories are of patchwork ladybirds, of soldiers, hawks, and then the sad tale of my cousin the dung beetle who lived in the northern hemisphere. . . ."

"Where my father lives? The top half of the world?

One day when I was a little girl at school the teacher held up an orange in front of the class and said, 'The world is round, like this orange; in fact, the world is like an orange.' Then she peeled it, and divided it to show how well it fitted together, but there was a green patch on one side where it had gone rotten, and then the juice squirted in the teacher's eye and she said, 'Excuse me' and left the room, and when she came back her eye was all red, as if she had been crying. . . . What is the matter, Uncle Blackbeetle?"

"You asked for a story. I am waiting to tell you of my cousin. I heard of his death from his sister who is literary, having been brought up in an apartment of dictionaries, and who is much traveled, having spent her formative years in an atlas of geology, soil distribution, mineral resources, land utilization, climatology, human distribution, natural vegetation, ocean currents, world communications—it is through her knowledge of the last that I am able to talk to you and tell you the story of my cousin's death. . . . Are you listening?"

Uncle Blackbeetle began his story.

"Why do I say 'my dear cousin'?" (said Uncle Blackbeetle) "I never knew him. He was a stranger to me, he spoke a different language, he lived in a different part of the world. Yet since I received the news of his death I have thought much about him and dreamed of him at night and wondered why he was toppled to death by his

173

treasure, with his mouth and eyes stopped up in the dark so that he could no longer see the sheep treading the path where he lived and watch the dung falling in drops of—is it licorice? Between lichen and life? Or a broader division —leveler and lock?

"In that part of the world, so I have heard from my cousin, there are tarns lying like shining blackbeetles in nearly every valley; bog myrtle grows, and bracken, common pilewort, and moss, stained violets and primroses; and the air is filled with the curse of the juniper tree. The cuckoo in spring spies, threatens, his voice a pendulum of sky, hanging nowhere, refused anchorage by the sun. My dictionary cousin has lived between anchorage and angel, with an anemone growing up through the cracks in her little house. Another cousin lived between dingdong and dire, which is a different story. But this cousin who died, Albert Dungbeetle, lived and died on the side of a sheep path within sound of the curlew, the raven, the water wagtail, the meadow pipit, and the grunt and cough of black-nosed sheep with curled horns. He lived within sight of tarns, juniper trees, fells, and, quite near his door, a scatter of empty pork-and-bean tins measled with rust.

"As you may guess, the concern of my cousin Albert's life was to bring home the dung to the little house where he lived in a dark hole in the earth. He had fine legs for the purpose, to clutch and roll, and sharp eyes to see the

174

sheep trotting by on the path. All day he hid in a bed of grass, watching, listening, ready to seize the beautiful dung as it fell from the sky, for my cousin Albert believed that his treasure was delivered by a god, it seemed to arrive to him from so far away, from such a height, from somewhere close to the sun and the stars. Sitting there in the grass all day, watching and waiting, my cousin had time to consider the question of gods and distance, and because at the same time he also considered the fact of dung being dropped from the sky, he united the two questions in his mind and gave himself one answer, which is more convenient, don't you think, for one has to economize and fit thoughts together, seam to seam, in order that they may not take up too much room in tiny heads.

"Now, or so I heard from my literary cousin, Albert became ambitious in his gathering of dung. He learned to reject the smaller pieces and to wait, sometimes for many days, until a heavy mass almost his own size rolled from the sky. He became obsessed with the idea of collecting a larger and larger ball of dung and sometimes days went by before he returned home; while his wife, Jenny, used to call anxiously from the door of their little house, 'Albert, we are so hungry and cold and lonely.' (She had, I think, three children at the time.) 'Albert, bring home the day's treasure and let us all sit round the hearth and be content.'

175

"But day after day Albert replied, 'Wait, wait, my dear. I am so sure that today a magnificent piece of dung will fall. I am prepared for a miracle. I am sitting here in the grass waiting to seize the Treasure of All Time when it falls from God.'

"Soon Albert did not go home at all. He stayed every night by the side of the sheep path, thinking about God and distance and stars and dung and listening to the sheep coughing and grunting and chewing, and watching the birds fly to their nests; and all the time he kept alert for the great occasion when enough treasure to last him for the rest of his life would drop near to him and he would reach out his hands and grasp it and twine his strong little legs around it, and draw it inch by inch to the house in the earth where his faithful wife and three children waited for him.

"Albert grew thin. He developed a tiny cough which made a stalky sound, like split grass, but nobody, that is, no human beings could have heard it, not above the sound of the sheep and the birds and the tourists passing in their cars and down all the hills the waterfalls leaping and crashing—do you know the waterfalls, Erlene? They curdle and spill and are called 'Sour Milk Force.' Their speech is so loud. They tape their white tongues, measuring the crags, reading their prepared speeches in the dark, from the damp clay tablets of earth.

"I know. My literary cousin told me, who lived between *speech* and *spell*."

"But that is where I live, too," Erlene told Uncle Blackbeetle. "Does that mean that I should be able to read the writing in the earth, and understand what the waterfalls are saying? Is that why I understand the speech of the beetles? Yet I myself cannot speak any more even though I live between *speech* and *spell*."

"So you do, Erlene. Or between *specter* and *spindrift*, between *spark* and *spirit*, *seem* and *sprout*, *seek* and *spy*, *seed* and *squander*, *science* and *stone*. It is a delicate matter to choose one's boundaries of words."

"But Albert Dungbeetle?"

"Yes. Albert. His health began to fail. His cough grew worse. He starved. His wife and family starved. Yet still he had the strength to wait all day and night by the sheep path in the hope that the huge bundle of dung would fall and provide him and his family with sustenance, pleasure, and memories, for the rest of his life. Sometimes as he lay in the grass, a spider or an earwig or a dragonfly or perhaps another beetle taking his tiny bundle home to his wife and family would stop and talk to him and ask him why he waited day and night by the side of the sheep path. He told them why. Some said, 'How foolish you are to stay out in the cold when you could be home with your wife and family, sitting

177

round the hearth, safe and contented.' Others said, 'How selfish you are, you do not think of your wife and family dying of hunger.' And others said, 'How brave and noble. What integrity. What patience. What stupidity. What intelligence, foresight, power, ambition.'

"And as the days passed and Albert grew older (and it was indeed a miracle that he was able to survive though he was starved and thin and his body was racked with coughing), all the other insects in the grass used to bring their children to stare at Albert, and again some would say how brave he was, and others how foolish and some asked how, if there was really a god, he did not look down from the sky and perceive that Albert was waiting for a wonderful piece of dung and drop it down to him out of kindness. Soon the children of the insects around were chanting rhymes about Albert Dungbeetle, poking fun at him. But some were afraid of him, and mothers said, 'Don't stray in the tall grass or Albert Dungbeetle will get you!' And if their children misbehaved, Mother Spider or Earwig would say, 'I warn you, you'll grow up like Albert Dungbeetle!'

"Yet a settlement of spiders in the district elected Albert as their counselor. Another settlement of worms, who are creatures not afraid to admit that they feed upon the dead, made Albert Honorary Dictator, and stitched a tiny flag, which on State occasions and public holidays and funerals was hoisted to the top of a stalk of grass where it flapped red and spotted like a lady-bird's wing.

"Soon Albert was such a familiar sight, sitting there cross-legged in the grass, that people began to forget why he was sitting there, and rumors circulated that he was a priest beetle, a mad beetle, a foreigner, a tramp, a god. Albert no longer talked of his reason for sitting there. Perhaps even he had forgotten why he waited. So many things happen in a lifetime, it is easy to lose sight of the original aim. One begins to wait for a different reason, for different objects to fall from the sky, and sometimes when the object one has longed for arrives, one does not recognize it, it is so long ago that one dreamed of it, or it does not conform to the dream shape and one would prefer that God had not sent it, that one should continue only to dream of it. . . . I know. My literary cousin lived between *dream* and *dunghill*, between *doxology* and *dwindle, division* and *duplicity*.

"Now it happened that one day Albert was sitting motionless by the side of the sheep path, with his eyes closed and his head rocking gently from side to side, and his shiny black body propped against a beam of sun, when he heard a rumbling sound from far away, from somewhere in the sky. The sound came nearer, and Albert opened his eyes and sat tensely waiting, though he could not quite remember what he was waiting for.

Then onto the sheep path, just near where Albert was sitting, there dropped an immense ball of dung. And Albert remembered. I imagine, though I do not know, but my literary cousin has explained a little to me, that Albert's first impulse, after rushing forward to embrace his treasure, was to cry out with joy, to tell someone of his good fortune, to speak . . ."

"Poetry?"

"I'm not sure. To speak . . ."

"With words, Uncle Blackbeetle?"

"Yes, Erlene."

"With words in a language, nouns, verbs, adverbs, sentences clipped like hedges and lawns into strange shapes that surprise you in the dark? Sentences with the growth cut back; or like wild bush where there's a struggle among the plants to get first to the sun? Words which climb other words and feed upon them or blossom on them, like clematis? Dim green sentences with yellow shadows? Sentences like greenhouses where the words wither at the first entry of a wind from the snow, but the flowers inside, pampered, never exposed to the weather, are exotic wonderful colors? Words, Uncle Blackbeetle? Like lighthouses? Words with their

180

beacons roaming the seas to rescue the thoughts or warn them against perilous tides, cross-currents, approaching storms? My mother talks of lighthouses, Uncle Blackbeetle. There is one on the coast, Waipapa Lighthouse, away down where the muttonbirds, the sooty shearwaters, fly."

"Muttonbirds, like sentences, live in burrows."

"And words like cabbages, Uncle Blackbeetle? Stout, full, wet?

"Like drainpipes blocked with dead leaves and mice?

"Like a feather from the breast of a bird?"

> "I crossed a moor with a name of its own,
> and a certain use in the world no doubt,
> yet a hand's breadth of it shines alone,
> mid the blank miles round about.
> For there I picked up on the heather,
> and there I put inside my breast,
> a moulted feather, an eagle feather . . .

"Well, I forget the rest. . . ."

"I know that poem, Uncle Blackbeetle, though I do not know moors and eagles and heather; only paddocks, manukas, matagouris, bracken, hawks . . . hawks. . . ."

Erlene started to cry. She made no sound in crying but the tears were running down her cheeks and onto the windowsill.

181

"What if the hawks come, out of the sky, Uncle Blackbeetle? Will you save me from the hawks, and from the soldiers in twos and threes?"

"You're a crybaby," said Uncle Blackbeetle. "A crybaby indeed. Now listen while I tell of my cousin Albert. Don't cry, Erlene. People who are brave enough to pick up eagle feathers on the moor don't cry and are not afraid of hawks. I know. Between *death* and *elder* there are *dragons* and *eagles;* between *havens* and *hell* there are *hawks;* that way the world goes."

Erlene stopped crying.

"Do you know the game, Uncle Blackbeetle?"

"Which game?"

"We used to play it. You say, 'This is the way the world goes round and somebody must touch.' And you close your eyes and you have to guess who touched you."

"Somebody must touch? How strange! Somebody must touch. No, I don't know the game. You only know a game when you need to know it. Time is passing quickly Erlene. I am quite dizzy at the way it passes, and I haven't yet finished the story of my cousin Albert. Do you want to hear it or shall I put on my apron and begin work?"

"Talk to me, Uncle Blackbeetle. Tell me the story."

"And you'll forget about hawks and the soldiers and you'll have that eagle feather tight in your hand?"

"Yes. Talk to me."

Uncle Blackbeetle coughed and looked about him and began rather self-consciously, "To continue the story of my cousin Albert Dungbeetle.

"So an enormous piece of dung fell onto the sheep path, and when Albert realized that he had been waiting day and night for such a gift from God, all his former strength and enthusiasm returned, and he prepared to seize the dung and roll it to the little house where his wife and children waited. He stood for a moment savoring the prospect of his treasure—the smell, the mighty size, the perfect shape and texture—then feeling in himself the power of fifty well-fed healthy dungbeetles, he advanced to his prize, clasped it in his arms and legs, and began pulling it toward his house. In spite of his sudden strength he found his task difficult, and after every two or three steps he was forced to rest, and the way seemed so long and unfamiliar with stalks of tough grass springing to strike at him and tangled roots obliterating the remembered landmarks. At times he struggled ahead without his burden, in an attempt to clear the path; other times he sank exhausted by the wayside and would have given up had he not thought constantly of his wife and family, how they were waiting for him, how proud they would be when they saw his treasure, and how they would forgive him for his desertion and

183

prepare a feast to celebrate the arrival of the treasure. And now as he drew nearer the little house in the earth he found the strength to sing . . ."

"With words?"

"Yes. Dungbeetles have words."

"Was it,

> "I crossed a moor with a name of its own,
> and a certain use in the world, no doubt,
> but a hand's breadth of it shines alone
> mid the blank miles round about. . . ?"

"No. Albert was not between *death* and *elder*, he was between *dream* and *dunghill*, where eagles do not fly.

"It seemed to take him days and nights to reach his home, and once or twice he was so tired that he fell asleep, and that was strange, because while he had been waiting for his treasure he had not slept at all, but now that it had arrived he could let himself sleep."

"Sleep, with dreams?"

"Yes. And at long last he arrived at the entrance to the little hole in the earth that was his home, where his wife and family were waiting for him, with a nice fire in the hearth, and a little table set with tiny knives and forks and spoons and plates heaped with piping hot dungbeetle fare. Albert's mouth watered at the prospect

184

of it! With a mighty heave he drew his treasure toward the little house, with his back to the door, then suddenly with a superentomological effort he entered the hole, pulling the treasure, which plunged as far as the door where it lodged and would not move. Albert peered about him into the darkness. How strange! There was no fire in the hearth and no table set with food piping hot. There was no one home. Albert called along the small corridor to the room where he and his wife used to sleep. There was no reply. And there was the magnificent treasure blocking the doorway and the light, and there was no one to be proud of Albert, to congratulate him and share his triumph and prepare a feast. At first he was going to sit down and weep, he felt so lonely, but he decided, No, I don't care if my wife and family have deserted me, I still have my magnificent gift from heaven, I will bring it into my little house, and sit beside it, and admire it and love it, for is it not the result of a lifetime's planning and watching and waiting?

"Then drawing a deep breath he stepped back, to make a run at the treasure and with a mighty heave pull it into the house. There was a crunching sound under his feet. He had trodden on a tiny pile of beetle bones and shells—the remains of his wife and family. He realized that he had sacrificed them for his treasure, but he was heartened at their faith in him. While he had

185

waited, they had been waiting. They had starved. Even after long days and nights when he did not return they had faith in him and did not leave the little house in the earth except perhaps to go to the door and scan the grassy path in the hope of seeing him arriving with the promised treasure.

"They would want me to take care of it, he said to himself. I will bring it into the house and cherish it, for the sake of their memory and suffering.

"Such is dungbeetle logic, Erlene.

"And now Albert began to shiver. It was cold and dark in the little house and the roof was leaking. Albert realized that his arms and legs were bleeding. There was no ointment or bandage and no one to bind his wounds. The little house seemed so dark. If only he could move the treasure from the doorway, for what use are treasures which block the sun? Albert tried to run at the treasure, but he fell panting on the little pile of beetle shells and bones, for all his strength had vanished. He tried to rest, and thought, After all I can still ponder my magnificent dung even if I cannot place it upon my hearth. But the house was so dark and lonely, and he did not want to stay there among the bones of his wife and children, he wanted to go out like a valiant beetle, and find a new wife, build a new house, where he would take his treasure to be admired. But his arms and legs

were bleeding. He kept coughing. He thought that perhaps he was dying. He was lying on his back now, staring at the terrible obstacle which blocked the light and
warmth from his tiny house. His treasure! A feeling of
hate was born in him. He hated his treasure. He could
not understand why God had dropped it from the sky,
why God had promised so much in a ball of gleaming
dung, why God had kept Albert waiting all his life with
dreams of the glory of his gift when, in the end, all that
it had brought was darkness and death.

"Anger gave Albert the strength to make a last effort
to pull the dung into his house. He attacked it, embracing it fiercely, and suddenly the dung was dislodged,
toppling through the doorway onto Albert and crushing him to death, so that he died imprisoned and
murdered by his treasure.

"I know. My literary cousin has lived between
celandine and *charnel house*, between *caul* and *cherry
red*, where *charity* lies, and when she called one day at
Albert's little house in the earth, to pay him a charity
visit, she found the roof of the house collapsed, the dried
ball of dung with maggots hanging up their lace curtains
in its windows, lying in Albert's kitchen, and Albert
pinned dead beneath his shriveled treasure. My cousin
gave one look through the gap in the roof, closed her
eyes to shut out the vision of the city of maggots with

187

the body of Albert as its foundation, and hurried away home, through the grass forests, along the sheep path, and down to the edge of the tarn where she lives under a baked-bean tin with her husband, a woodman by trade, and their youngest son, training already for the dung heap. And that night, by the light of the moon shining on the tarn, she wrote to me about Albert's death. She did not know, she said, the strange workings of a dungbeetle mind; she lived, she said, in fear of her son's future. She even warned me—me! I am no dungbeetle! —about the danger of being imprisoned and murdered by the object of one's love! My poor literary cousin! She told me she will never forget the sight of Albert sitting cross-legged by the sheep path while the neighboring insects played near him, teasing him, quarreling over him, carrying flags in his honor, begging him to sign treaties and petitions; and the visit to his home where a populous housing estate of death has sprung from his body.

"Is that fame? Should I mourn Albert? I am not familiar with the ways of dungbeetles and only know what I have been told by my cousin who for the sake of her husband's trade has moved to a forest in the neighborhood of *flock*, *flood*, *foliage*, *forgiveness*, and *fountain*, which is only a short distance from her son's place of work in *faeces*, *faerie*, *fantasy*, and *fact*."

With a deep sigh, Uncle Blackbeetle took his apron,

pinned it around his waist, gathered his tools, and began once again to work, while the sun shone on the window-sill and two legless handless sightless worms crawled from a crack in the sill, to lie in the sun.

"Talk to me. Tell me more stories!" Erlene pleaded. "Don't start work now. Soon it will be winter, and you know that in winter you will go into your little house and stay there with the blinds down and not come out and talk to me. My father is coming to visit us in winter. He has wonderful lists of people, trees of people with leaves and fruit and rings of age. He is preserving the human race in syrup, heavy syrup, but the weight on the container is false, and nobody realizes. My father has promised to save us, that is why he went away and left us, so that he could return and save us. Do you suppose that he knew Albert Dungbeetle, that he arranged to drop Albert's treasure from the sky? My father is very powerful. Did Albert have a funeral? My grandfather had a funeral and we put jam jars of flowers on his grave. My head aches with speaking. Once I thought dust was sunbeams but now I know it is dust. Once I thought that if you crooked your little finger and wished with your best friend, your wish would come true. Have you got a best friend, Uncle Black-beetle?"

"I can't talk anymore to you just now," Uncle Black-beetle said. "I'm going to keep an eye on your father when he arrives. What manner of man is he, again, your father?"

"But Dr. Clapper said that!" Erlene exclaimed in astonishment. "Why are you speaking like Dr. Clapper?"

Dr. Clapper leaned forward and smiled a smile of triumph. He seemed so excited that he forgot to arrange his writing paper and run his finger along the edge of the hospital pen.

"But I *am* Dr. Clapper," he said. Then he frowned as if perhaps there were some doubt; but he banished the frown with another smile, and repeated, almost as if trying to convince both himself and Erlene, "But I *am* Dr. Clapper. And you have just spoken to me, Erlene. We won't talk anymore today, but I'll tell your mother you are getting better by"—he hesitated—"by leaps and bounds, or shall I say like a house on fire or like nobody's business or in double-quick time or with giant strides?"

Erlene was silent. How could Dr. Clapper manufacture coffins from a hospital pen? And where did he keep the dead beans who lay with their one black eye closed forever? Why was everything so strange and shifting? And why had nobody cleaned the windows? —the raspberry blood still stained the glass. And the room was still divided, with enemy territory beyond the desk, and with the door as her special property, with freedom to go in and out, in and out. She wondered if it had been wise for her to insist on control of the door; for doors are a responsibility; they take charge; people are ushered, in spite of protest, in and out of strange places.

So Erlene escaped. She ran to the door, opened it, and ran home. She did not wait for her mother. She ran along the top of the hill past the laundry and the Nurses' Home, down past the frog pond, through the fence, up the drive, across the bridge, and home, into her bedroom where she shut the door and went to the windowsill in search of Uncle Blackbeetle. He was nowhere to be seen. Perhaps he is resting, she thought. He looked tired when I last saw him. Yes, he is resting.

She stood with her eyes closed, counting, waiting for Uncle Blackbeetle to finish resting. He will come out soon, she thought, and talk to me. He will tell me another story. She waited. She heard her mother coming home from the hospital. Her mother opened the bedroom door and peeped in, with a joyful smile on her face though she said nothing—why? Her mother closed the door again while Erlene sat by the windowsill until she might hear Uncle Blackbeetle stirring from his rest, yawning, putting on his apron ready for work. And awful fear began to grow in her mind that Uncle Blackbeetle was Dr. Clapper in disguise, trying to get at her and spy on her and tell her stories by pretending to make coffins on her windowsill. Yet she had known

Uncle Blackbeetle before she met Dr. Clapper . . . perhaps he had changed to Dr. Clapper . . . perhaps it was Uncle Blackbeetle up at the hospital and that was why he had not appeared now on the sill, because she had hurried home too fast for him to put on his disguise?

Her head ached with trying to decide and arrange. And still Uncle Blackbeetle did not appear that day or the next or the next, and Erlene sat lonely and silent keeping vigil, with no one to protect her from the soldiers passing in twos and threes or from the hawks flying down at night.

Her mother struck her across the face, pressing her lip across her teeth so that her lip was pierced and the blood trickled down the corner of her mouth. "Speak!" she cried. "For God's sake, speak! I've had enough. You've got to speak. We're all doomed if you don't speak. I and you and your father. The whole world is doomed. Please speak to us, Erlene! And now tell me what you said to Dr. Clapper today—why won't he tell me what you said. I don't believe you spoke to him; you would speak to me, wouldn't you, if you could?"

Erlene wiped the blood from her face. It was not raspberry blood but a brighter red, like dahlias, but her mother did not seem to be noticing the color of the blood, she was staring at her own hand as if she could not believe that it belonged to her; then a cunning expression came into her eyes, as if she were trying to devise a punishment for herself, for her hand. It seemed that she found the right punishment. The limb was imprisoned, chained, and would not hold food anymore or touch furniture or pick the dahlias and the early plums and apples and the Bon Cretian pears; it would not hammer on all the locked doors, trying to get in, or button clothing to the neck, or make shadows; it would no longer arrange, wave, protect, beckon, strike, caress; it would not write.

A look of fear came into her mother's eyes.

"I'm sorry," she whispered. "It's that I'm in my room, writing, and you're in here, withholding information."

I know, Erlene thought. You want to torture it out of me. You want me to reveal the names of my accomplices. You think that if I give you a list of my accomplices you will be saved. You are like my father. He thinks that a list of one family will save him—and the human race. You believe that lists are magic. Or perhaps it is something else—a crime, and you wait to be accused.

Her mother was staring at her.

"What made you do it in the first place, Erlene? What made you decide not to speak?"

Tell me, she was saying. If you tell me the culprit I will make myself responsible for the punishment.

And she means, Erlene thought, If you say that I am the culprit you know that I shall kill you.

But I cannot speak, and my blood is like dahlias, not like raspberries or cherries, and my stain does not spread upon the windows of enemy territory. . . .

"I thought," her mother was whispering, "I thought some kind of sudden act, a shock, might help, and that's why I struck you, Erlene. I did really believe, you believe that I believed . . ."

On the shelf of belief the ironed faiths are folded and warmed for putting on when night and winter come. Remove one belief and all topple and crease.

She is clairvoyant. All God cares about is genealogy, getting the generations in order until the end.

She is pregnant, by Uncle Blackbeetle. The relationship is disgraceful, disgusting.

So the beetles crawled out of all the holes in her body, and unashamedly in the sun they set up a city, an estate of death, for the ultimate treasure was too terrible and fearful a burden.

"We're getting on nicely," Dr. Clapper was saying. "A word here, a word there, perhaps next time you come, soon the story will be pieced together and we'll know the criminal, we'll find out the culprit. But if you say, Erlene, that I am the culprit, you know that I shall kill you, as I killed the fly on the windowpane.

"We're getting on so nicely. I'm sure that by and by you'll have so many secrets to tell me."

Night came, and next morning Erlene found Uncle Blackbeetle's body on the windowsill. He was cut in two, as if a chopper intent on dividing, dividing, had fallen out of the sky. Unless it was the beaks of the hawks? The tears ran down her face and onto the windowsill, and they made rainbows, for the sun did not know, and she could never tell it.

12

The voices nagged him at night. They disappointed and shocked him, for he had always believed, as people do, that if ever a voice from a cloud addressed him it would be concerned with prophecies, eternities, that it would provide remarkable information which man had been unable to get in any other way. Except for one or two occasions, Edward's voices talked trivialities, telling him, for instance, that the door was shut when he knew that the door was shut, that he had forgotten to pay his paper bill, when he knew that too. Or they called his name, not, as one might expect, as if he were a chosen soul hailed from the heavens, but as if he were being called to lunch by someone who did not particularly care if he stayed hungry. At other times the voices spoke ob-scenities about the Strang family; indeed it was mostly the Strang family who featured in the remarks; but again they told Edward nothing which he did not already know or suspect, and this infuriated him with a sense of wasted time, for he could not decide whether he should listen to the voices in the hope of collecting a stray prophecy, or whether he should ignore them and seek revelations from people who had not such a need to remain bodiless, who could be answered back and argued with and whose speech could be made visible and human, though less effective, by gestures and the stacking of sentences, in picket patterns, between flesh and light. Yet however he decided to act, Edward could not ignore the voices. They claimed his consciousness as if it belonged to them by right. They occupied it entirely, and only when they had withdrawn could he make some movement, or attempt to reply to them, and by that time it was always too late; they had fled; he was left alone, angry, ashamed, confused, and often afraid. The Strangs, they said. The Strangs.

Ridiculing them; making fun of his life's work for the human race.

He had answered the letter from Clara Strang in New Zealand. Yes, he had said, he would visit her in Dunedin. He wondered why he cared to visit, after his encounter in Prudence Avenue, Peckham. He had written to Vera of his plan to visit New Zealand. He had booked his seat on the plane. The voices kept worrying him. In the evenings now when the battles were fought, none of the soldiers would accept a medal for bravery. Edward hired the woman who typed his files to clean the blood from the battlefield; the two had made love, only once; she understood; though he suspected that at night she cried big muddy tears and in the morning her nose was stuffy and the soles of her feet hurt, as if she had been stamping on stone.

Each evening there was so much blood on the battle-field; there were court-martials to follow, men set before a firing squad.

And Edward grew more restless and tired. His eyes troubled him. One of his teeth ached. The Strangs, Edward. The Strangs. And Erlene has lost her power of speech; the enemy is advancing in your own family, Edward, your defenses are pierced.

Now the woman who typed for him (Magda) had returned from her annual holiday and spent each evening with him. She wore that orange blouse and those black beads and her skirt was short and tight, up over her knees that were huge, like smoothed blocks of wood. She fussed about Edward, bringing him wet packs for his jaw when his tooth ached, and lotion for his eyes when the unsummoned tears ran down his cheeks, and all the time she gazed at him with a longing which did not find its way into her speech—she made gay, bantering remarks, "You great baby, how can you hope to go on living without someone to look after you? Do you know you've sat there all evening without a break for coffee?"

Then she would make him a cup of coffee, pampering it from the moment she put the milk in the pot, brooding over it until it was almost boiling, tenderly arranging the two cups in their saucers, and when he sat drinking it, not speaking or glancing at her, still absorbed in the battle or the voices, again Magda spoke lightly to him in the manner she had adopted since the one night when they made love, "You're quite inhuman, Edward. When you're working or dreaming you're quite inhuman."

That pleased him; it was a way of escape, a way to get rid of his concern for the human race and the name Strang Strong Strange estrange danger extra, but were people anagrams after all? Words and speech—he went to the park, the gate was pulled to, He was found to be insane, Was he, I think that there is a mistake, That is the reason I am here, shape pleases, sob bitterly, rat trap, a "kembed oration will cost both sweat and rubbing of the brain. . . ."

The answer, the voices told him, is a chair. At first he laughed Ha ha ho ho, and then he understood the message. He was human. He would design and make a chair for himself, to fit himself perfectly, to be molded to the shape of his human body; and he would sit in the chair, reading his books, considering the Strang family, and his disillusionment at meeting the living represent- atives of it; and when he returned from his flight to New Zealand the chair would be waiting for him and again he would sit in it, as a human being, and recall his meeting with Clara Strang of Dunedin, his meeting with his wife, and the marvelous way in which his visit had prompted his daughter to regain her power of speech and utter prophecies. He wondered why he had never thought of making himself a chair, why he had so readily accepted the furniture provided for him by landladies. He realized that in all his life he had never known a chair which allowed him to sit and think and dream and work without intruding its physical presence—its hardness, lack of comfort, its ease; broken springs, barred back, layers of antimacassars fighting against the stains of flesh and sweat. It seemed to Edward that he needed desperately and immediately a material impartial object to contain him, and as the time did not seem ripe (though it may have been) for either a cradle or a coffin, he chose to design and build a perfect chair.

"I'm going to make myself a chair," he said to Magda the next evening, after he had packed away the toy soldiers and put the current file on the Strang family into its correct position in the cabinet.

"Until I leave for New Zealand I shan't be needing these."

"Not the soldiers? Who will spill each day's necessary blood?"

"I shan't need the soldiers."

"What about the Strangs?"

"I am not concerned at the moment with the Strangs. I am going to build a chair."

So all day and in the evenings now he was thinking of it and at night he dreamed of it; somewhere to sit, to

200

direct his life, himself, and the world, a throne, a little house, a safe place from which to consider the prospect of civilization and its triumph or ruin, a place of immunity, inaction, the body disposed of, layered skin to cloth to wood, the feet stopped in their restless pattering up and down the sun-deep wall-to-wall planet.

He became more serious and short-tempered and Magda slaved to do his bidding, trying to interpret his instructions while he sat with his naked back pressed against the cardboard mold which she measured and arranged and removed. While he was absorbed in the making of his chair Magda stayed with him, sleeping in his bed and putting the camp bed for him in the kitchen, preparing his meals, seeing to his washing, encouraging him when he cast aside designs which did not please him, and at night waking, perhaps in fear, when she heard him trying to catch the voices as they withdrew beyond the range of his reply—his abuse, argument, entreaty. During this period the idea of the chair occupied Edward entirely: it seemed to have replaced all thought of his approaching flight to New Zealand and what it promised or threatened; all work with the Strang family, and the memory of his visit to Prudence Avenue, Peckham and the fact that he seemed to have been accepted as a member of the family, provided he did not inquire too closely into murders committed (strangely enough) by white white sheep. Yet once or twice Edward remembered Vera and Erlene. Vera, he thought, is beyond my reach; she is bound by that strong sun-colored raffia which resists all weathers, which never splits or breaks a thread. If I had stayed with her living as her husband she would eventually have changed me into a mountain or a stream or a tree, for she possesses that power and whim which the gods took great delight in—the metamorphosis of human beings into natural scenery. How many husbands have only to try to escape and their wives promptly turn them into stones or trees! No man has ever been flesh to Vera—he has been air, earth, water, fire.

He thought of Erlene—her loss of speech and how, as soon as he saw her again she would break her silence, not with cries or moans but with new articulate language which would replace the derelict words washed up on barren islands of the mind and sprouting rank poisonous growths of time and use. We depend on Erlene, Edward thought. We depend so much upon her to speak for us. Is it privilege or revenge that the opportunity to speak a new language and the threat of eternal silence have entered my life? We have asked so many things and people to speak for us—like the waves, we knock our foreheads against the shore, pleading for the word; we listen to the syllables of nonsense uttered by streams and birds and trees and by the objects we ourselves have built and made tenants of our lives, all in the hope of discerning the message placed between the layers of babble. Is it possible that Erlene, my daughter, can deliver the language we long for?

Then once again the dream of the chair would intrude in Edward's thoughts; at night he was conscious of sawdust accumulating in his clothes and mouth and eyes; his eyes stung and watered, and his face was pale, yet his body seemed to be growing plump, in a distressing way, as if it were trying to defeat his aim, as if it were trying to overflow the bounds placed upon it by his design of his perfect chair. I'm getting flabby, Edward thought. A glance in the mirror disturbed him. Yes, flabby, pale, the truth is beginning to come out. Ha ha. Who from his throne will save the world? Between cradle and coffin is not a throne the most suitable container for the human race? Men must be kings, even if they are flabby pale men who try to save their lives by clinging to a mediocre family that cannot confess its acts of murder. For the Wallace Strang who had been tried at the Old Bailey and who had been the subject of so much denial in the letters Edward had received, had been executed only a week ago, and still nobody had owned him, no next-of-kin had come forward—not Smiths or Browns or Petersons or Bradleys or Wilsons or Stewarts or fellow Strangs. Or Glaces.

He was no relation to me, Edward thought. If he had been, then I would have claimed him, admitted the relationship, but oh no, he was not *my* brother or cousin or uncle or father or son.

And on the night of the execution Edward had gone to sleep early, drawing the Strang dream over him like a blanket, as protection for him against all people and all families everywhere; safe for the time being, yet waking again in the morning to the truth and deeper dream—the knowledge that with one twist of language, as with one throw of dice, the brother father uncle cousin stranger would be juggled and spun and the blood-spotted *brother* lie face upward to confront him.

In the States, he thought, they sit people in a chair to kill them. It is an annihilation of the dignity of one of the most civilized postures of man, the place where his imaginings of cradle, bed, coffin, are given articulate form; it is true, I believe it to be true, that chairs burst spontaneously into flame; painters have seen it happening, and have set down the image of it; one of the loneliest men who lived has shown faith in the continuance of humanity by painting the stark and fitting dignity of a chair.

So day and night Edward was obsessed with thoughts of chairs. At times he was appalled by the vanity which had led him to build a chair for his personal use, to fit his body only. He remembered the bay in New Zealand where he and Vera had picnicked, and the huge throne of rock that someone had built on the shore, in order to be able to supervise and command the waves. The same man had also made a castle overlooking the bay.

"He is locked up now," Vera said. "It does not do to make castles and thrones."

Edward remembered that he and Vera had tried out the throne, taking turns to sit in it and shout commands at the heedless Pacific, which went up and down its own blue scalloped path, licking at the shining black rocks and laying its cheek softly on the warm sand, making ministering nurse-movements dressed in its cap of white foam.

"It feels wonderful, doesn't it?" Vera had said "to be sitting in a throne, even if the waves take no notice. I wonder what it is like on the left or right hand of God? You should know," she added, he remembered, with bitterness.

He replied, "Wonderful; trying to make him change his mind and let me manage the affair; also trying to get him to clarify the exact position."

"The throne is fine," Vera repeated. "But it doesn't fit."

"No," he said, squatting on the smooth stone seat and gazing at the sea, "it is too spacious for one person. There is always room on a throne for one or two more, a companion, man or beast."

"But the man who built this," Vera reminded him, "is locked up now. Perhaps he sits on the floor somewhere, in a corner of a small room with no view of the sea."

"No," Edward said. "He still sits on his rock throne, and the waves obey him though he speaks very softly now, yet he speaks in their own language . . . what is it, Vera?"

"Nothing. We can't even fit into the things we make. How can we be expected to fit into what lies around us, fashioned long before our birth?"

"We could try making chairs instead of thrones. . . ."

"And lose the opportunity to sit on the right or the left hand of gods?"

He made his chair. He could hear Vera saying, "I can't understand people who give up their ideal of changing the ways of the world to fit the men who live in it, and try to satisfy themselves by making cradles, chairs, beds, and coffins to contain one person alone—themselves. Yes, Edward, even double beds contain only one person at a time; there are alternating flashes, like traffic lights, to warn and entice the mystery.

The chair was perfect, he thought. He could work and dream in it. He realized that he had never possessed anything which fitted: clothes seemed to resent him, and shoes pinched; even his skin was not quite at home upon his flesh. He longed to be wearing an artificial limb. He envied people whose flesh and blood could learn to live in such apparent harmony with wood or metal. He had a cousin, he remembered, whose head had been shot during the war, the top of his head quite sliced off, and the surgeons had replaced it with a metal cap which would sit there for the rest of his life, like a precious lid to his dreams. But the metal had been an invasion: the cousin, on the advice of his insulted brain, never learned to accept the metal cap; therefore he had grown strange, he laughed a lot, at the wrong time, in the wrong situations.

"Things are serious," people said. "Things are dead serious; there is nothing much to laugh at."

No, Edward thought, there's nothing much to laugh at. But what kept troubling him long after his chair was made, and long after he had finished wondering at the impulse which had forced him to set aside even his research on the Strang family, was the amount of sawdust which gathered, increasing each day, in the room and on his clothes, and in the street shedding itself in his footprints, and sifting from his sleeves when he leaned on the table in the library; and it seemed to remain in his throat, next to his voice, penetrating it; and when he walked and one of those anonymous winds which spring up in the street, blowing from nowhere to nowhere, swirled about him, its burden was not leaves or scraps of paper but sawdust, clouding about him almost as if his body were a tree with a circular saw at work, secretly, within him.

The voices told him it was Vera's doing; she had changed him into a tree.

He rejected that explanation. He divined that the ominous dust represented his unity with his chair. Yet he did not know, he did not know, sometimes he dreamed, and he wondered where he had been living all the time he was making this chair that was not even a throne although (and because) it fitted the shape of his body. He began to think once more of the Strang family, of his journey to New Zealand, of Clara Strang in Dunedin; of Erlene who would speak in the new language.

I must try, he said to himself one night, while real tears ran down his cheeks, I must try to understand metal and wood and people, and all the paths, and the executions for the murders I have committed, and the placards I must carry, like laundered handkerchiefs, against the end of the world.

All the same, I will choose to sit with a beast upon the throne.

And soon it was summer, and the sun came out, shining on North London, and the lilac bloomed, and the wallflowers and the roses, and the pregnant women walked up and down in the sun, and Edward left one night, like a thief, for London Airport and his flight to New Zealand.

13

Everything is prepared now for Erlene to speak. We await the arrival of her father. Dr. Clapper has said that during one of his interviews she uttered a few words, but he tells me this with an air of jealousy, secrecy, almost of fear, and in a threatening manner as if I am forbidden to believe that she has spoken. He implies, in some strange way, that Erlene's words have convicted me—or him, or others—of such guilt that it would be in my own interests not to ask for details. The child herself remains silent, often sitting by the windowsill, with tears running down her cheeks. What can I do? Should I seal the room and pretend that Erlene has gone away or is dead, and leave her there alone forever, letting her starve and die in silence? Should I refuse to admit Edward when he flies in, wax melting, having tasted the sun, carrying his sole offering to me, his pocketful of Strangs, which he will take and spin upon the table, like coins, to show me how rich his life has been? But he will part with none, oh no, he will return them to his pocket, clinking the generations to remind everyone, especially himself, that he is so involved with humanity that he fills his cloth and flesh pockets and pouches with the worn blackened bent or new-minted currency of people. And I shall not be able to get close enough to him to find out if the coins have been defaced, the identifying image rubbed away.

His plane arrives next week. He talks of staying with a Clara Strang of Dunedin, but when it suits him he will visit us, traveling north by train, and I shall meet him at the railway station, standing on the platform carrying out that futile police-searching of faces, so ready to pounce and pin the guilt of identity upon the criminal, and hoping against hope that no one recognizes me also as a criminal, another of the plundering league of people who break and enter anonymity in search of model faces and eyes and bodies and slants of mind leaning, like bean stakes, against the moss-grown walls. But we are not the only criminals; on my many secret ventures to steal and stock myself with myself I have been surrounded by faces, eyes, limbs, begging to be stolen, to be set free of their prison of anonymity. How I smile to myself in the daylight when I note the assumed innocence of people and remember those secret smugglings, woundings, murders, that take place away out on the edge of being where the one-track wind blows from the regions of death, and people are struggling always for their identity, trying to carry home in knotted handkerchiefs, handbags, purses, brain cells, gutters of flesh, those parts of themselves which they most treasure; but in the dark there is always confusion, with pieces of self being mislaid or exchanged unawares or snatched by others who covet them, so that on return from the outer edge of being there is little cause for triumph; the entire plunder has become the common property of humanity.

But names, we have names. I shall search for Edward, tall and dark-haired with his dark-rimmed spectacles; his youthful air, his absorbed smile; his nervous movements; no, he is not thin, for his face is plump in a way that does not quite match his body, as if he carried a hamster compartment packed with pieces of torn— words? Certainly not food. Paper, people? The fullness in his face makes me curious to know the contents of his extra store. His eyes, I remember, glint like newly deposited tar that has not congealed and needs barriers arranged about it to prevent people from venturing near and being branded with great black stains that will not rub off or wash out. And always there is this concerned air about him; I know that he is genuinely trying to rescue the world from destruction, yet the sublimity of his purpose is at times so diffused by his human frailty that his attitude of involvement seems a mere pose of panic, as if he were a weak schoolmaster trying to control a classroom of rowdy children, as if he were not so much interested in his control of them as in the fact that he might be dismissed from his post if the headmaster walks in to confront him with his inefficiency.

Yet all the time I am thinking of Edward I know that I am being betrayed by Change. It angers me. I have always been indulgent with Change: he has shared my house, my food, my bed, the people I love; yet when I am dreaming in this way of someone I have not seen for so many years, Change refuses to comment or help or offer advice. He could tell me so much by pruning my dreams to allow the truth to grow out of them as a prized and shocking blossom and fruit. But Change says nothing; he too knows that his power lies in his silence. . . .

So I shall stand on the platform of the railway station among the discarded sandwich crusts and the sea-gull droppings, with the near sea snuffed strong in my nose, and glimpsing out of the corner of my left eye the gray tower of the gasworks with the spindly spiral ladder encircling it, and no one standing on the ladder or climbing it: I have never seen anyone climbing it. I have often thought I should like to go to the top and gaze down into the cylinder; I do not know what I should see. In my mind the gasworks is always the repository of unwanted animals—cats, dogs who are sick or too old, and people: I hear in the night the mysterious clanking sound which tells that people are being borne away and put to sleep within this gray tower. . . .

The train will come fussing in, and stop, and I shall

move out of the way while the passengers make their stampede for the refreshment rooms, and when they are all appeased with their drinks and buns, I shall look for Edward. How strange and absurd—shall I wear a veil? I shall be without Erlene. Dr. Clapper, again with that air of jealousy and secrecy, has advised me not to take her when I meet Edward, but to have her prepared to receive him when we arrive home; that she should stay in her room and await him there. I confess that I am afraid. I dread that Erlene will make some remark to incriminate me, and no matter how deep my actual guilt may be, I need to preserve my seeming innocence. I no longer hope to rival my daughter's silence by ridding myself of light and sound, of the smell of gorse, of snapdragons, moss, empty sacks, closed books, of those rusted gratings in the earth through which the dead peer, momentarily, and where rotting leaves cling and saliva dribbles from the foaming mouths of manic detergents trying to remove the habitation stains of people from the earth. I no longer hope to rid myself of the stirred smell of light, inseparable from dust, as the unseen wind blows and the footsteps pace up and down up and down unsettling the sleeping arrangements of chalk and soot and sand and seed grains. . . .

Yet I do not know how much longer I can bear the silence in the next room. It seems to have spread like an influence, to the whole house, to the furniture which I love and never thought to speak to, yet now there are moments when I demand speech from it, not the occasional sharp snap-crack of wood bursting its bonds of space, easing itself in the hot dry weather, nor groaning whining responses to the wind blowing under the door and against the walls of the house, but articulate language, the unique speech of furniture. Lately I have found myself suddenly hammering with my fist upon the table, here, where I write this, or upon the panels of the door, as if a gesture of violence may help me to break into the silence of everything around me, to ransack and spill the words which lie trapped there. Other times I have stroked the furniture, touching it gently as an archaeologist may caress a newly discovered piece of stone, knowing that in the end, if it is cared for, it will give up its secret, it will speak its language to him.

It has occurred to me that perhaps Edward too has lost his power of speech, that when I meet him he will stare at me as Erlene stares now, proclaiming my guilt, that he will go to Erlene in the next room and sit with her and the two will remain there forever in silence. And gradually others will join them. People will call at the house, enter the next room, sit by the windowsill and contemplate the insects, all in silence. The whole world will be struck dumb, and I shall be the only one left with speech, and all will gaze at me, proclaiming my guilt and not replying or seeming even to understand when I speak to them; but they will smile and smile amongst themselves in their new secret language; and everywhere I go—I cannot go far, for this town and this country are my loves—I shall find heaps of decaying words—on the sides of the road, in gutters, in rubbish dumps and litter tins, for every home will have cast out words as useless, throwing them recklessly and thankfully away yet without thought for hygiene, forgetting the stench and diseases which arise from accumulations of decaying or dead words which no one has taken care to bury or burn. How can I take it upon myself to be responsible for the language of speech if the world is struck dumb? Oh, I must urge the furniture to speak, and the walls, and the trees; my clothes, my food, all objects must speak; it is a panic; anything to drown the final silence of the human race! What use is the silence? Even now as I look out of the window I can see the mounds of rotting words, the foul steam arising from them as, like compost, they generate their own fertile vapors and powers . . . you see? there is no end, growth must emerge from them, perhaps I too shall walk all over the land scattering the dead words upon the soil and watching for the plants which grow from them, all the new trees which will shelter us from the sun and the fires in the sky. It is a new Eden: the growth of articulate speech from the silence that fell like a shroud upon the language.

My body seems to have stopped its living; yet my mind is carried forward, on and on. The people are dumb. They are dead too, lying in the streets. The houses are empty. Day after day I hear news of refugees crossing the border, fleeing from the plague and persecution of silence, and in their anxiety setting up house anywhere throughout the inarticulate cities governed by Mumble and Mutter—Mutter!—while the beautiful birds fly overhead with more meaning in their brief sharp cries than the doomed human race may ever again utter. It has sometimes been the fashion to keep birds near us, trying to train them to imitate and thus preserve a little of our meaningful speech, preparing ourselves for the time when we shall be silent. We have been so patient with these birds; we have kept them in roomy cages, fed them with vitamin-charged golden seed, provided them with mirrors where they can make love to their images and abolish their loneliness; and day after day as our silence threatens and, like the encircling sea, floods through the inlets of our speech, we have tried, perhaps as our last hope, to teach these birds our meaningful language. Surely there is hope for us when our little yellow birds can swing back and forth on their tiny swings and whisper with their tiny voices, "Pretty, pretty, Jack and Jill went up the hill, pretty boy, Mary had a little lamb its fleece was white as snow!"

217

I met Dr. Clapper in the street this afternoon. He has aged suddenly; I swear that his hair has gone gray. He looked guiltily at me. He seemed afraid.

"It's not long now, is it?" he asked.

"No," I said.

Then he hurried on his way, seeming to glance about him for fear that he was being observed, and I took my usual route to the Public Library, but I was afraid to go in, for I was alarmed at the placard in the window—SILENCE; it seemed larger than usual, and more ominous. I was reminded of the first line of an old rhyme we used to chant as children, "Silence in the Courthouse."

But I am innocent. How can I convince the world that I am innocent?

14

So Uncle Blackbeetle was dead. She was truly alone now, at the mercy of the soldiers and the hawks and her mother and Dr. Clapper, and soon her father. She noticed that Dr. Clapper had moved his table a little nearer the door, encroaching upon her territory, and that two more flies had been killed and their blood was splashed upon the windowpane, although it was wintertime now and the lives of flies and their secrets should have been sealed by frost. And now Dr. Clapper had grown increasingly cunning, standing sometimes like a salesman at the door of her sleep, handing out free samples, smiling gaily, his grassy hair flattened glossily over his forehead.

"No obligation to buy," he said.

One night he gave Erlene his body, free, provided that she return it afterward, parceled with the correct postage, but she could find nothing to wrap it in and no string to tie it and no stamp and all she could find was Uncle Blackbeetle's apron, which she wanted to keep for herself forever and not to give to Dr. Clapper, but he snatched it from her and tied it around his body and the next day when she woke and went to keep her appointment with him he was wearing the apron instead of his white coat.

"I have a cousin," he was saying. "Do you know my cousin?"

But Erlene was silent. There were four dead flies on the windowpane where so much blood was spattered that she could not see through the window to the outside world; and now very little territory remained for her: almost her only possessions in the room were two feet of floor space and the door. She ran her fingers along the wall of the room, hoping to find secret panels or passages which she could claim, but she found none. And all the time Dr. Clapper moved nearer, smiling, gay, his fingers full of thorns from his pen where he had rubbed his hand along the holder to prove that he was human. "See, I am human, I am rubbing my hand along the holder!"

Sometimes Erlene wanted to go to him and offer to remove the thorns, but that would mean crossing into his territory, so she merely stayed her side of the table and stared at him and was silent. It was raining every day now, with brooms of mist brushing through the sky and foam floating on the surface of the creek, and when Erlene and her mother walked through the long grass to the hospital her mother kept saying in a voice more afraid than ever, "Our ankles are quite damp; soaked through."

Her mother had never struck her again or pleaded for her to speak, though sometimes she questioned her, "Did you really say a few words to Dr. Clapper? What were they, my dear? What did you say? Tell me, Erlene. What did you say?"

But Erlene remained silent. Now that Uncle Blackbeetle was dead there did not seem to be anyone to trust, and certainly there was no one to speak to, and though Erlene walked up and down the paddocks, up the hill by the plantation of gum trees and pine trees, along the road by the saleyards and over the next hill, she never found an eagle feather to put inside her breast; only, once, she picked up a torn sodden paper-and-paste wing that had fallen from the sky. And that, she said to herself, must have belonged to my father. He has set out from the other side of the world and has been lost and forced down into a paddock full of strange cattle who have devoured him, flesh, bone, skin, and left only one torn paper-and-paste wing. His journey has been a failure; he forgot to make treaties with the powerful sky.

One evening when Erlene was returning from the bathroom past the open door of her mother's room she noticed her mother with her fingers to her ears; she was putting something inside her ears. Her mother saw her, and flushed, and spoke out sharply, "Why don't you speak? Why don't we just sit down together like ordi-

221

nary people and speak? I'll say something to you, and you reply, and I'll reply to your reply."

Her mother's voice grew more gentle.

"That's the way people talk to each other, Erlene. Have you forgotten? I'm alone in my room just as much as you are alone in yours. And I'm so afraid of the silence that I have bought these little wax protectors— see? (she held one for Erlene to inspect)—to put in my ears and defeat the terrible commotion of quiet, only to give myself peace of mind in this last week when we wait for your father . . . he has arrived in New Zealand, Erlene, he is visiting a family in Dunedin . . . I believe. . . ."

Erlene wondered what her mother believed.

"Yes," her mother went on, "only to give peace of mind until your father returns. And you'll remember Erlene"—her voice was pleading now—"that one person speaks, another replies, another replies to that reply. There are words to use, so many words. Don't you remember all the wonderful words in all the books upon your shelves—the shelves that Grandad made for you? Grandad would like you to speak.

"Look, now."

Erlene's mother removed the wax protectors from her ears.

"Look, I'll come to your room, and sit down with you, there by the windowsill though it's dark outside, and we'll talk, just this night and every night before

222

your father comes to us, and I shan't tell a soul what you say to me, no I shan't tell Dr. Clapper or anyone." Then suddenly Vera Glace leaned towards Erlene's silent staring face, and gazed at her with eyes full of a strange dread.

"You think you're the world," she whispered. "You think you're Death and the dead. You think we're going to follow your example, that you can silence the entire world by your not speaking, that you can in the end shut up even the smallest noise of being—the faint swish of the stars, of grass, the echoes of the human brain. You think you are omnipotent, beyond words, beyond the need to walk up to people and speak, and for them to reply and you to reply to their reply, all in the safety dance of speech, touching syllable to syllable. . . ."

Then Erlene's mother began to cry, with her face gawky and red, so that Erlene felt sorry for her, but she was not really a mother for her red flesh had holes in it, like wire netting, and it smelled like an empty cage where the only creature that she had cared for and fed three times a day had escaped or was dead, lying in the corner; her mother was an empty nest spattered with the remains of people who had flown away or had fallen out and broken their neck or their heart or been pecked to death by the hawks. Her mother was still crying softly. Then with a sudden glance of fear around the room, and a swift panicky movement, she thrust the ear protectors back into her ears, and shutting the door of her room she returned to her desk, and Erlene heard her crying for a long time while outside the opossums scratched at the trees with their sharp claws, and Erlene remembered that opossums had been known to tear out the eyes of people who had surprised them in the dark. One had to be forever on guard, watching, listening; one did not dare stop up one's eyes or ears. Why didn't her mother understand that two pink little balls of wax were no ammunition against silence or sound or light or darkness?

As she lay in bed listening to her mother's sobbing she wondered if it were true that her father was Adam sitting at his desk in the Garden of Eden, totting up the generations, gloating over them, trying to preserve their future by making lists of them, so many lists and notes neatly typed and stacked upon his desk while he leaned over them, encircling them with his arms, cowering beneath the sky for fear of being addressed by "ancestral voices prophesying war." Ancestral? Lumbering beasts who cannot speak with words, whose library, like the Lord's Prayer, can be contained on a threepenny piece of metal or space—room for the same episodic grunt snort snarl, chapter by chapter, tinily, the feeble interpretation of morning, sunlight, hunger, fear, love. Was her father so afraid that he would be addressed by a beast?

And what was the secret of her mother's fear, which drove her to stop her ears with wax? Were the menacing voices already traveling nearer and nearer, and that was why her mother sobbed in the next room and her father had set out in panic flight from a great distance to silence the Strangs in Dunedin, to silence all voices which might threaten him? And why did Dr. Clapper so often sit at his table, not speaking, his head on one side, listening, listening?

"Speak, speak!" her mother had said.

Perhaps they were waiting for advice, for love, for commands, for explanations which they thought she might be able to give them. Then why were they so afraid? Erlene remembered that when she was very small and learning to walk, there were wooden bars, like a cage, set up around her, and her mother and her father and her grandfather stood outside the cage and stared at her. They were so tall. Their mouths dribbled with saliva, and their shadows pounced, one shadow upon the other, along the ceiling as they leaned over the wooden bars. Was it something she remembered? Erlene wondered. The faces moved, and the shadows moved with them, and words came out of the faces, sharp, commanding words, "Walk to *me*, Erlene, walk to *me*, walk to *me*."

And her mother and her father and her grandfather stood gazing bitterly at one another, and then turning to Erlene to plead, "Walk to *me*, walk to *me*, walk to *me!*"

And sometimes they held before her, trying to entice her, good things to eat, bright new toys, a rag doll with curls down to its shoulders.

"Walk to *me*, Erlene, walk to *me*, walk to *me*."

But she had stayed safe inside the cage while the shifting shadows fought, blotted, wounded each other on the ceiling.

It was something I dreamed, Erlene thought.

And now it was her mother, Dr. Clapper, and soon her father trying to persuade her to speak, and why couldn't she speak any more? Why was speech of no more use to her? Had someone—a god—in trying to make an exact pattern of her to keep in dusty archives in order to make sure the pattern was never repeated— had he smeared her with a strange substance which ought to have set and been removed, as a model of her, but which stayed forgotten, congealed on her skin and her life, imprisoning her, acting as a soundproof wall through which, even if she uttered words, nothing could be heard, no cry or sentence or poem . . . ?

It was many and many a year ago
in a kingdom by the sea
that a maiden there lived whom you may know
by the name of Annabel Lee.

Nothing she uttered would ever reach anyone's ears; the words would merely beat themselves against the wall, and failing to penetrate it, they would circle her skin and grow old and stale, and cluster like flies about her, and lay little white eggs upon her, as if she were dead; or they would turn upon her, and in revenge for being unable to reach beyond the wall where people were waiting to receive them, they would attack her, with knives and stings and swords, and in the end devour her, so that when the god who had forgotten—why had he forgotten?—to remove the pattern from her, at last remembered her, and came to her, and tenderly separated the stiffened case from her body and her life, he would find nothing within, only a heap of dead word-wings and the stale smell of accumulated sentences and phrases; and no trace of a human being.

But perhaps she had changed now, perhaps she was no longer a human being, and when she spoke at last it would be as an ancestral voice, the voice of the beast, that would make her father tremble with fear and clutch protectively at his carefully compiled generations; that would make her mother hurry to find the little pink wax balls to stop her ears from the true sound rising at last from ice and marshland, ancient rock and stone, the ultimate denial of cities and people and rich stores of language skimmed century after century from the settled civilizations of human beings.

Was that the reason her mother and father were so afraid? Was that why Dr. Clapper was afraid and why he had begun to wear Uncle Blackbeetle's apron—in order to be able to say, when he at last heard the voice of the beast—"But I knew, I have lived so long in the earth, in ancient rock and stone and ice and marshland. . . ."

It was all so strange. Erlene's head seemed dizzy with trying to understand; the sun was curdled in her head and an inexplicable wind kept blowing round and round, following arrows, trying to get out of the maze. No one had told her but when her mother began talking of the Strang family and her father's interest in it, of his visits to the family and the friends he had made, then Erlene knew that there were no Strangs, that her father was a myth and a dream, that he would never return, and that neither she herself nor her mother was real. It seemed as if the three had one night been given free passage in the world, emerging in the path of a dream from the mind of someone asleep, and preparing to fly on and on, as dreams do until they slowly dwindle to snowflake-size and nothing, when a strange guardian of the night had pounced upon them, seized them, forced them to account for their identity, in a way which dreams have no means of doing; they had been threatened, imprisoned as human beings, and denied their rightful blissful fate of dissolution. . . .

Was it true that soon her father would visit her?

Was he flying like a god through the sky to visit his creation? Would he bully her into speech? Speak, speak, Erlene! Would he show jealousy because she remained the other side of silence?

Lying in bed, not sleeping, her confused thoughts forming and breaking and evading one another, Erlene tried to find stillness as well as silence, she longed for a frost to visit her head and to set, like plaster of paris, upon her broken thought, so that it would stay quiet and still, and then, when the bonds of frost were melted, her thoughts would be healed again, firm and complete, fitting one into the other like wheels, sunflower wheels. . . . The 'possums were striping the bark of the trees with scars. Venus was shining just above the horizon. The cold Southern Cross leaning above the world was half-shadowed in a crucified darkness where the quarreling winds lay in wait snatching at the torn garments of cloud. . . .

Erlene thought, If only I were dead, if only I were lying deep in stone with the pattern of my life shining against the light, if only I were not Erlene Glace who cannot speak, who has nothing to say, who is so far away from the world; Erlene Glace who used to go to High School wearing a badge in her panama hat and another badge on her navy-blue blazer with the red braid; who used to sit side by side with the other girls in school listening to Miss Merchant reading poetry,

229

"Avenge O Saint thy slaughtered bones.
Men are we and must weep. . . ."

Thou hast left behind powers that will work for thee, thou hast great allies. . . .

Poetry . . . mathematics, arranging triangles and circles, stepping with the piercing feet of compasses across the pages "Ruled feint with margin" . . . shining torches fitted with cheap unreliable batteries into the dark dusty places of history . . . or, if history were to be compared to a raging ocean reticent in its discussion of the drowned yet hysterically claiming and snatching the occasional bones washed up on the shore which bounded it . . . did not Erlene and her classmates use to sit in Miss Merchant's classroom, in imagination approaching the historical ocean, formally and shyly, as if they undressed their minds each in its private striped red-and-white bathing machine, and creeping down, ashamed and secret, to meet the waves and retrieve one or two bones from the store of the drowned?

Did it happen that way? she wondered. If only she were sitting now in her desk at school, in the sixth-form room, turning the pages of Shakespeare, shutting the words face to face with those on the opposite page, leaving them a moment, then separating the pages and observing the stain of creation where word had joined word, blood had been shed, and the letters were lying

230

tangled and asleep, bounded by their dark cages upon the cloud-white paper.

And yet, Erlene remembered, the sixth-form room was at the same time filled with terror, and all could feel it when week by week news came that one of the girls—in turn Molly or Beatrice or Helen—was planning to leave school, or had left already to take up nursing or to work in the Farmers' Coop or the post office. . . . But they all stifled their terror and smiled to each other and said, What fun, I wish I were out in the world earning . . . like Molly and Beatrice and Helen. . . .

But Erlene was going to attend University, she was going to be a student, listening to lectures, reading, wearing an old raincoat and flat-heeled shoes and not caring at all about her clothes or makeup, and not because she couldn't afford to, but because she was far removed from the ordinary concerns of the World. And in the University city she was going to walk up and down the streets till late at night, thinking about Plato and Socrates, trying to solve the problems of being and not-being, hand in hand with Death. She was going to be a Buddhist, she was going to believe in free love, she was going to be an atheist, writing pamphlets which would cause her to be dismissed from the University; and perhaps in the end, not understood, tramping alone through the streets and then wandering alone on the beach, she would be drowned, yet not in New Zealand, not in any of the bays there—Waipapa, Moeraki, The Picton Sounds—but somewhere in the Mediterranean, off the coast of Florence while sailing alone or with a lover who said . . .

"Emily, no, *Erlene*, a ship is floating in the harbor now,
A wind is hovering o'er the mountain's brow. . . ."

It was that, you see, it was that, and the eagle feather and her father ticketing the generations.

Now the time was between two and three o'clock in the morning and Erlene began to feel afraid, for it was the time when people died, when hearts stopped beating, at first just for experiment, then growing used to the silence and stillness they stopped beating forever; when the world was seized by a frost that was not the graceful white lace drapery revealed in the first timid light of early winter morning but a stark lethal frost originating in human bone and flesh, created by man himself. Now was the time, she had heard, when the spider-web hammock of will-to-live upon which old and sick people rested, swinging under the darkening sky and above the dark abyss, was prone to loosen its hold and snap; when the spun desires for light and warmth died at last or feigned death with the result that the web was never mended, a new one was never woven, and the old and sick people with the broken threads of their collapsing desires encircling them dropped useless into their waiting graves; just like so many stale loaves toppled from a string bag.

Between two and three o'clock in the morning was also the time when dreams refused to be drowned, but floated accusingly within sight and sound of the dreamer; when the heart slowed in its beating, packed in sand, heavy, like a sack of pipis brought in with the tide and stranded when the tide went out, as tides do, hanging placards on the shore for the comfort of those who haunt beaches who keep returning again and again to make sure what the tide is up to, what gifts it has strewn on the sand, whether it is at home, in bed, asleep, complaining, raging, raking up the past or the dead, letting the matter rest, avoiding the issue, or whether it has got tired of sitting brooding on the cheerless hearth and has put on its green cloak and gone out to do destruction—murder or love. . . .

But I don't know about love, Erlene thought. Love is the Scholar Gipsy and my mother and father and the sound of the trees at night.

And what about Dr. Clapper, snipping pieces of everyone and trying to fit them upon himself, wearing disguises, running in and out of people as if they had no power to resist him, as if they were water instead of walls, and why didn't he understand when Erlene tried to tell him with secret signals that people were stones and castles and prisons and it would take a bomb to get them to open the front door one inch; and that one could not so easily remove the skin of people as if their minds were buckets of boiled milk only waiting to be skimmed and skillied, adulterated, diluted, changed? But Dr. Clapper was powerful. She had spoken one sentence to him, she was sure, though she could not remember the details of it, and yet he had told no one, not even her mother. And lately while the soldiers in twos and threes were passing through the sky and the hawks had become so brazen that they now perched on the windowsill where Uncle Blackbeetle had lived and worked, Dr. Clapper seemed not to be aware of the warning signals; he seemed preoccupied with the arrival of Erlene's father, and he kept saying to her mother, "It will work wonders I am sure Mrs. Glace; I have a feeling that when her father walks into her room and they recognize each other, then words will come quite naturally to Erlene, her speech will return as if she had never lost it in the accident."

Which accident? Erlene wondered. There had never been an accident, except of birth. There had been school and lessons, tennis and basketball, singing in the choir, preparing for exams; and at home her mother crying and knocking on the furniture to be let in or to

234

release whatever was locked there; and across the other side of the world or in the sky her father writing lists of people in order to rescue the human race from extinction; no, there had not been an accident, there had just been a time when the human race grew up suddenly and panicked at the sight of the empty sky which they had once filled, for comfort, with fat old men wearing beards and smiling blue-eyed smiles and dropping promises that disintegrated when they reached the atmosphere; no there had never been an accident; but words had turned, all the timid words had turned, and now no one was real—not her mother or father or anyone. What had come over them? Why were they all now mere calculations, adjustments of silence? They were no longer people. They were tiny pieces torn from a vast white sheet of *blotting paper*, and flicked across the face of the earth. They were all silent now. Sound was absorbed into them, staining them, blocking their thoughts and their dreams, not able to leave them; the pent-up weight of words had fallen; the world was at last muffled by the drifting centuries of its own speech. There was no longer need or power to speak. There was only sleep left, numbness too deep for dreaming; the cellulose culture; the nerve ends permed and lacquered like unmanageable hair; there was only Death, with the everlasting words falling and melting, people and words, paper and snow, piling in great drifts, con-

cealing tracks and roads and railway lines, cutting off
communication; words falling all day and night blocking
the doors of speech, and what use was it for people to
proclaim themselves people, for the Scholar Gipsy to be
the Scholar Gipsy, leaving his Berkshire moors, Bagley
Wood and Godstow Bridge and "warm green-muffled
Cumnor hills" and emigrate to New Zealand, wandering in the paddocks and bush, the King Country, the
shores of Wanaka and Wakatipu, Waikaremoana, Half-
Moon Bay, Waipapa, Fort Rose, to sit idly by the
unsympathetic Waitaki that was absorbed in its own
snow-fed fury, or listen to the magpies on the banks of
the Rakaia, or roam (wearing his "outlandish garb")
as beatnik up and down the North and South and
Stewart Islands, waiting for the spark from heaven
when all the world knew it was too late for fire, unless
it was the kind which enabled the soldiers to fill their
sachets with people ash and disease, which forced her
father to invent the Strang family in the wild hope that
it would survive, as dreams may be known to do, when
all else is destroyed, which confused her mother to the
extent of inducing her to blackmail furniture and to
weep by the grass-grown beds of rivers that consulting
no one had changed their courses and without the usual
patronage of willows, flax, rushes, were taking the
unplanned lonelier route to the sea. The Scholar Gipsy
could wait forever now. No fire would fall from the

236

sky; no God would descend to comfort his silent people. Only day and night the ideas were falling in drifts of sound, words, human cries, piling against the houses and the walls of the cities, shrouding the whole world in silence; there was no reason to speak anymore, there was no power to speak. How could anyone speak unless the new language were discovered in time?

Therefore Erlene closed her mouth tight and turned away when the unfamiliar fat man with the bald head and the rimless spectacles opened the door of her bedroom at half-past twelve on Thursday of the following week and said, quite softly. "Erlene, speak to me Erlene.

"Don't you remember Uncle Blackbeetle?"

15

"Show Mr. Glace your spelling book, Jimmy. Go on, open it!"

Impatiently Clara Strang snatched the book from Jimmy, opened it, and spread it upon the table for Edward to admire.

"I'm coaching him," she said. "Look at that page, and look at this, before he came to live with us. I coach the three of them, I make them do their lessons every night. You have to stand over them. I brought up my girls the same way. I put them to dancing and music and elocution although I've been a widow for so many years, and now here I am taking in orphans from the Children's Homes; being a foster parent; a lot of gratitude you get, and a lot the authorities pay for the upkeep, I must say! but it's in me, I'm a born mother. I know how to bring them up. Now Peter here—say hello to Mr. Glace, Peter"—Clara turned to Edward and spoke in a loud whisper—"a wet bed every night, every single night, but I'm teaching him; the only cure is to rub their noses in it. Tommy's the best so far, good as gold, not a peep out of him, all his lesson books put away neatly in his room there. . . ."

She went to the door of the living room and opened another door beside it in the small passage.

"See, their room."

Edward looked in at the three small beds placed around the wall. Jimmy, Peter, and Tommy, who had just come home from school to find this strange man visiting their foster mother, stood uncertainly in the doorway holding their exercise books and their well-worn navy coats. Edward thought they looked unhappy and afraid.

"But you came about the family, didn't you?" Clara Strang suddenly reminded Edward and herself, and turning to the children who cowered before her and stared up at her with their big brown eyes, she said, "Remember, change your clothes. Tommy, you see they change their clothes. And before you go out to play there's your piece of bread and jam each in the scullery on the table. Say good-afternoon to Mr. Glace."

Jimmy and Peter and Tommy gave Edward a quick glance and did not speak but hurried to their room to change their clothes.

"Poor little devils," Clara said as she showed Edward back into the living room.

"I do my best for them but they've got no family. They get spoilt in a Children's Home. I never spoilt any of my own. Now Mr. Glace."

They were sitting facing each other. Clara Strang was tall, huge in build with a mighty, attached bosom, and a small head, sparse straight brown hair flecked with gray, and a pale soft face which changed shape with her every expression. Her mouth was a small O but her voice filled the room and she swayed as she talked, like a massive tram rocking on secret tramlines to the terminus.

"It's curious isn't it?" she said, "that you're interested in the Strangs, and here I am taking in orphans and waifs and strays. It's in the family, this social work. What have you discovered about the Strang family, Mr. Glace? You know of course that the murderer is no relation to us—Wallace Strang. They hanged him, I believe. I read about it in our papers and in that *Daily Glitter* or whatever it is, one of the neighbors has it sent from England, it's got headlines like undone bootlaces, and it had about Wallace Strang. I said to myself, Thank goodness I'm living on the other side of the world or people might gossip, but of course when you live on the other side of the world you're out of the way, aren't you?"

"Yes," Edward said. "But I'd take care if I were you."

Clara Strang looked puzzled.

"What do you mean?"

"It's nothing," Edward said. He laughed. "I try not to get the lines of human reference tangled, otherwise I get my families mixed. Have you a copy of *Who's Who?*"

For a moment Clara looked overwhelmed; then she gave a gasp of delight.

"You don't mean," she said, "that we're in *Who's Who?* that we're *someone?*"

Edward was abrupt.

"No."

"Then what do you mean? I accept your credentials of course because they're signed and sealed, and I've invited you into my home because of your interest in the Strang family. What have you discovered about us? Do tell me! Are you going to write a book about us? I'm only a Strang by marriage but our children are Strangs—there's Noeline getting married next month to an accountant, he's studying it. I've never met a genealogist before. What do you do exactly?"

"I have just made a chair," Edward answered. "Not long before I left for New Zealand I made a chair. There's really no time for me to go into details about the Strang family. . . ."

"A chair?"

Clara Strang seemed puzzled, a little afraid.

"The chair . . . I'm afraid Mr. Glace that I really must get going about my work, there's the children's tea, and their lessons to be gone through . . . poor little orphans, I don't get paid much but I take them in all the same, and I'll train them to be good citizens, we haven't enough good citizens have we? You said you'd like tea, just a cup? I really haven't the time you know."

"Of which city?"

241

"This. Dunedin. Here, Quarter Street St. Kilda. I'm not looking any farther afield than Quarter Street St. Kilda and don't condemn me for it, for I can see that you've got your little boundaries too, Mr. Glace. I wondered about you, what your work was like; I somehow thought you would come here with charts and everything neat with red ink and asterisks, and I'm still not quite sure, but fancy, you've spent so many years studying us . . . fancy. Do you have people of your own, Mr. Glace? Just imagine, all the way from England, all those thousands of miles because you're studying the Strang family!"

Clara Strang looked thoughtful. It occurred to her, but she did not say it, that there was money in genealogy, for fares overseas were no laughing matter, and here she was, a widow working from dawn till dark to keep herself and pay the rates and the electric, and having to take in orphans simply because of the kindness of her heart, while this Edward Glace flitted here and there from country to country enjoying himself . . . who paid him? she wondered, who was he working for? and why? There must be something more to it, she thought. No one would take such an interest in an ordinary family like the Strangs . . . but people did queer things . . . that man from Nelson who had to do with atoms, it was said he spent all his time with them, that he treated them like people and they spoke to him, and he spied on the way they behaved. . . .

Oh no, there was not going to be spying on her in the Strang household!

"I don't know," she said, answering the summons of the kettle boiling in the kitchen; and then spreading a lace tablecloth upon the table ready for afternoon tea.

"I really don't know that there's much I can tell you about the Strangs. We're just an ordinary family. Gifted, of course; I put my youngest to the violin—it's still in the front room, in its case, a brand-new violin."

She looked across at Edward and repeated, "I don't know. I don't often entertain strangers. They'll be curious at work when I tell them about you. I hope Jimmy and Peter and Tommy don't get the idea that you're their long-lost father come to claim them! Although I've trained them to call me Mother, they understand that they're no relation to me; I'll explain that you're no relation as well, not to me or to them. They're funny kids, they can't quite get the hang of the idea that some people are just not related to other people, that some people's business is just not the concern of others. . . ."

She looked meaningly at him.

"You really have no right to come here, have you? I had hoped that I could put you up, as I said in my letter, but there's the children, I've always got children from

243

the Home now; but I've changed my mind—I understand your interest, mind you; I've got a brain and I use it—the eldest got her gifts from me, she's a window dresser now, employed by one of the biggest firms in the city; there's not much on display now because it's winter but you should have seen the windows in spring, all cherry blossom and little yellow chickens in among the blossom and daffodils . . . everything to do with spring . . . a lovely sight. . . ."

"I'm sure it was," Edward murmured. He had almost finished drinking his tea and he had eaten the collapsible white cake she had passed to him. He felt that it was time for him to leave. He wondered again why he had been so obsessed with getting in touch with the living generation of Strangs. Quarter Street St. Kilda was little different from Prudence Avenue Peckham—though there was something here, what was it, a sound all the time in the distance as of something raking and shuffling. . . .

"The sea's near?" he asked.

"Down the road," Clara answered. "It's not for bathing, there's an undertow; you can hear the sea everywhere."

She seemed to be listening.

"Yes, it's close," Edward said.

"Oh yes, it's close," Clara affirmed.

Edward put down his cup, scooped the white remains

of the cake, which crumbled, like fingerprint dust, into the saucer. He thanked Clara and assured her again of his interest in the Strang family, and asked that if anything came to light he would be so grateful if she communicated with him.

"If anything comes to light?" she repeated, gazing outside at the darkening winter afternoon and the snakes of mist rising, swaying and charmed by—by what?

Edward did not tell her; it was the piping of silence. The three children were standing by the gate when Edward went out; they were flushed with playing chasy and swinging on the gate, and their eyes glowed. They stared at him curiously. Then one of them let out a high-pitched cry which did not mean anything but was the sort of cry which little boys like to make in order to startle people—in trains and buses and closed places like Worlds where everything must be in order and voices must be kept low intelligible and civilized.

A feeling of panic came over Edward as the other two took up the cry.

He hurriedly turned the corner of the street, out of sight, but the children's cries persisted.

"There's no meaning in them," he told himself.

Then he heard again the raking shuffling sound of the sea, a burial sound as if it were filling in caves and graves exposed only by its perpetual need to uncover, reassess, and rearrange the dead.

It's time for Erlene to speak, Edward told himself. We cannot struggle any longer against the silence and the strange frightening sounds which have no meaning; we must have words, the new language of mankind.

Erlene will speak it for us.

16

"And that," said Dr. Clapper to the newly appointed psychiatrist, "is all I can tell you. We're trying to modernize conditions here, to step up the changeover in the treatment of mental patients. We're going into each person's case thoroughly for you so that you'll be able to set up the research unit and get to work with these modern treatments. Soon the wards should be half-emptied. We have little idea of what goes on in the head of that one, over there, and I repeat that all I can tell you is her name—Vera Glace, and that she has no family, she has never been married, she has been without speech for thirty years. God knows what dreams they hold inside them, what secret silent dreams lie like irremovable stones at the bottom of their minds, mixed with the sediment of their lives! If only we knew! She was a librarian I think, this Vera Glace, living in one of the small South Island towns, never venturing beyond her hometown, living, I suppose, a harmless sort of life; and then suddenly, at the age of thirty, she was struck dumb. No treatment that we have been able to give her has been successful. She has no family left. Curious, the turn of events."

"And of the screw," put in the newly appointed psychiatrist.

Dr. Clapper laughed, a little uneasily. He had been working hard in the past few months and had experienced some disturbed nights, troubling strange dreams which persisted during the day. He did not dare mention the fact, but he had got out of bed three times the previous night to go and study a blackbeetle that had found its way onto the windowsill. He hadn't killed it or brushed it into the garden below. He had merely got out of bed three times to study it, to memorize the reality of it. Ridiculous behavior, he had said to himself. It's the result of working fourteen hours a day, week after week.

"Yes, strange, strange," he said. "Glace is quiet, sheeplike; she is fed and toileted at intervals, her sleep is unbroken. We can't get a thing out of her.

"She won't speak," he added, rather sharply.

The newly appointed psychiatrist looked at him thoughtfully.

"Thirty years without speech is a long time. Poor devil. So, as you say, she squats over there in the corner of the yard, and God only knows what goes on in her head—if anything does, if there is anything human remaining; it is a cause for speculation. . . .

"Oh, she's human all right," Dr. Clapper said, again sharply.

"Who knows?" his colleague answered. "Human, animal, insect—spider, dungbeetle, blackbeetle . . ."

Dr. Clapper smiled mysteriously. "Ah, blackbeetle. I have a blackbeetle on my windowsill, no doubt studying the chain and turn of events."

"Haven't we all a blackbeetle on our windowsill?" said the new psychiatrist. "But, seriously, I would kill it if I were you. We don't want rivals you know. As for Glace, we'll get her to speak, in a few months she'll be chatting away nineteen to the dozen. Have any of the patients made friends with her?"

"Not exactly friends, but Matron tells me there's one, also quite withdrawn, who sits by her all day and sometimes fends off an occasional attack upon her. The two follow each other everywhere, but Vera Glace is the one who has to be cared for. I think if anything happened to the other patient—Clara Strang is her name—Vera Glace might get worse, her life might be in danger. In fact, if Glace were a savage and not a civilized human being she would spend her time saying prayers for her savior, Clara Strang. But she's not a savage, no no, of course not."

The newly appointed psychiatrist sighed.

"How do we know?" he asked. "How do we really know? But we'll have her talking, in the end. A shriveled little spinster of sixty pouring her heart out in the English

249

language, providing us with information that has eluded us for so long,—who knows?—perhaps throwing new light on the human race, giving us the final answer to the Problem . . . the breakthrough . . . hope for humanity, the future. . . ."

"You mean out of the jungle and into the clearing where the wild beasts are sitting in the sun?"

"You were always a bit crazy yourself, Dick. Any plans for that new job after your holiday? If you come back and visit us I've an idea you'll find my patient talking, you'll even be able to hold a conversation with her. Now that the ward has been broken into smaller units we'll be able to get together with our patients, to gain their confidence. I've no doubt you'll find the little old woman talking. No family, did you say? No husband, family, ever?"

Dr. Clapper shuddered.

"Her only human possession is Clara Strang, who tucks her in bed like a mother, who combs her hair, ties her shoelaces on the occasions when she must wear shoes. In a way Clara Strang is her sole means of survival. It's true. Vera Glace would die without her. Two torn people grafted together in secret life and growth. But if she does speak, is it worthwhile to spend so much time trying to get her to communicate? There are younger patients, more hopeful cases; you're still short of staff.

And what could Vera Glace have to say, after so many years of silence?"

The new psychiatrist laughed.

"Don't worry. She won't incriminate you. She won't point you out as the guilty party."

Dr. Clapper smiled nervously.

"You're in the mood for joking; I'm not. I'm tired, dead tired."

"Well," said the new psychiatrist when they had walked from the observation post out into the garden and twice round the snapdragon beds while the wild cries and screams of the yard patients echoed in their ears "you come back in three months and I'll give you the opportunity to hear your little old oracle talking."

And when Dr. Clapper returned in three months, just one week after the atom bomb had been dropped that destroyed Britain, and the world was still numb with fear, tasting people ash in their mouths and trying to whitewash the falling skies, he saw in the new small-unit ward, in the dayroom, Vera Glace sitting on a chair after thirty years, looking human, and speaking the language of humanity.

Dr. Clapper frowned. It seemed unintelligible, but he moved nearer to catch the new language. He heard it clearly.

"Ug-g-Ug. Ohhh Ohh g. Ugg."

Out of ancient rock and marshland; out of ice and stone.

————

The Women's Press is a feminist publishing house. We aim to publish a wide range of lively, provocative books by women, chiefly in the areas of fiction, literary and art history, physical and mental health and politics.

To receive our complete list of titles, please send a stamped addressed envelope. We can supply books direct to readers. Orders must be pre-paid with 50p added per title for postage and packing. We do, however, prefer you to support our efforts to have our books available in all bookshops.

The Women's Press,   34 Great Sutton Street, London

JANET FRAME
Faces in the Water

'I will write about the season of peril . . . a great gap opened in the ice floe between myself and the other people whom I watched, with their world, drifting away through a violet-coloured sea where hammer-head sharks in tropical ease swam side by side with the seals and the polar bears. I was alone on the ice . . . I traded my safety for the glass beads of fantasy'

Faces in the Water is about confinement in mental institutions, about the fear the sensible and sane of this world have for the so-called mad, the uncontrolled. Banished to an institution, Istina Mavet lives a life dominated by the vagaries of her keepers as much as by her own inner world.

Janet Frame's clear and unforgettable prose startles and evokes. A remarkable piece of writing by New Zealand's finest living novelist.

'Lyrical, touching and deeply entertaining'
John Mortimer, *Observer*

Fiction   **£3.95**

JANET FRAME
Living in the Maniototo

Winner of the Fiction Prize, New Zealand Book Award,
1980

Janet Frame again offers us a richly imagined exploration of
uncharted lands. The path is through the Maniototo, that
'bloody plain' of the imagination which crouches beneath the
colour and movement of the living world. The theme of the
novel is the process of writing fiction, the power, inter-
ruptions and avoidances that the writer feels as she grapples
with a deceptive and elusive reality. We move with our
guide, a woman of manifold personalities, through a physical
journey which is revealed to be a metaphor for the creative
process – on which our own survival depends.

'A many-layered palimpsest of a book, probably as near a
masterpiece as we are likely to see this year'   *Daily Express*

'Try it: it could change your unconscious'   *Evening Standard*

'Puts everything else that has come my way this year right in
the shade'   *Guardian*

Fiction   £3.50

MERIDEL LE SUEUR
The Girl

'If women are to get anything you have to be a guerilla, a thief, a tricker, a clown. O Lord, to be a woman!'

The Girl is an extraordinary piece of political literature. Set in the 1930's, it tells of a farm girl, who comes to town to work in a speakeasy. At a time of violence, repression and little hope, the girl and her lover fantasise that a future exists for them. Unemployed, he turns to strike-breaking, and then, desperate for money, the two of them join in an attempted bank robbery. *The Girl* is the story of a whole generation whose life was a struggle for survival; yet it is outstanding for its lyricism, its sensuous prose and for passages which convey real joy in life and in sexuality.

'Powerful, witty, lyrical, harsh'   *New Statesman*

'*The Girl* conveys harrowingly the narrowness and humiliation of a life of poverty, but this bleakness is mitigated by tenderness, humour and hope. Read it'   *Gay News*

'A book full of courage and wisdom, the most moving and politicising thing I've read in a long time'   *Spare Rib*

Fiction   £2.50

ALICE WALKER

Meridian
You Can't Keep a Good Woman Down

A major novel and a collection of short stories from the new wave of black feminist writing. *Meridian* is the story of Meridian Hill. Bitterly poor, she is able to get to college, but drops out to help Civil Rights workers in a voter registration drive. In her journey to rediscover her black heritage, loyalties shift and comrades change paths, and Meridian strives to reconcile the public language of politics with the personal language of feeling and emotion. *You Can't Keep a Good Woman Down* explores the prejudices of modern America in fourteen stories about love and lust, fame and failure, illusion and disillusion.

'Alice Walker again establishes that she is a cause for gratitude, delight and celebration'   Tillie Olsen

'Alice Walker is both so delicate and precise a writer that, instead of making ritual obeisances to conventional wisdom, she presents a beautifully rendered account of a personal life ... The movement of her imagination exists, pre-eminently, in the clear-eyed inspection of the human will'   *Sunday Times*

'A tour de force'   *Time Out*

'To read these books is to confront a life experience absolutely contiguous with the political issues of racial and sexual oppression ... To read them is an inspiration for women and men of any colour'   *New Society*

'A remarkable reading experience ... beautiful, complex and very sharp'   *Morning Star*

Fiction   *Meridian* £3.95
              You Can't Keep a Good Woman Down £2.95

TONI CADE BAMBARA

The Salt Eaters

Velma Henry finds herself in the Southwestern Community Infirmary facing Minnie Ransom, fabled healer and vehicle of the spirit world, when, falling on hard times, she tries to commit suicide. In facing the responsibilities of health so that she can become whole she delves, with the salt eaters – the black community – into the shared dreams of their past to find a shared vision of the future.

'A book full of marvels'　　　　　　　　　　　*The New Yorker*

'Swirling, whirling and compelling'　　　　　　　　　*Guardian*

'Toni Cade Bambara's magicians are women. Their words will bathe you in illuminations, and spread balm on bruised spirits'　　　　　　　　　　　　　　　　*Morning Star*

Fiction　　　　　　　　　　　　　　　　　　　£3.50